FLIRTY PUCKING WOLF

PARANORMAL HOCKEY LEAGUE

JENNY FENSHAW

PROLOGUE – TREVOR

New Year's Eve

Sighing, I snag a champagne flute from a passing server's tray and take a sip as the countdown starts. This will be the first time since I was fifteen that I ring in the new year without a kiss. I guess every streak has to end sometime. I'm twenty-five now, so that's ten years. That's a good run. Earlier in the evening, I danced with my best friend. The loneliness disappeared then. It always does when we dance and steal the spotlight, all eyes on us. I thought maybe I'd kiss her at midnight. Nothing romantic, we don't think of each other like that. Just a peck on the lips, one friend to another. But she's wrapped up in another man's arms now.

Whatever. It's just a kiss. As much as I enjoy kissing beautiful women, the streak I really care about maintaining is my point streak on the ice. Only hockey matters, not my hormones. New Year's Day is a fresh start, and I'm beginning the year as a professional hockey player. That's a dream I've had since I was a boy. I never thought it would be possible since shifters aren't accepted in the professional leagues, but now that the Paranormal Hockey League exists, we finally have the opportunity.

Out of the corner of my eye, I notice a delicate hand reaching out to grab a flute of champagne. I glance down into the face of a knockout blonde smiling up at me. She's tiny, even in heels. She's close to a foot shorter than my six feet, four inches.

"Seven, six, five…" The crowd around us counts, keeping pace with the numbers flashing on a giant screen behind the stage where the band sits. She takes a sip of her champagne and raises a light brown brow at me. I'm not sure if it's a challenge or an invitation shining in her stunning blue eyes.

I decide it's an invitation.

"…two, one. Happy New Year!"

As the band plays "Auld Lang Syne," I lower my head and kiss the beautiful woman standing next to me. She stretches to meet my lips and rests her free hand on my chest. I was right—it was an invitation I saw in her crystal blue eyes. I've just slipped my tongue into her mouth, tasting the lingering champagne and the ambrosia that's all her, when she pulls back and joins the revelers gathered in the ball-room of the Devil's Den Casino. She's petite, and her sexy bronze dress looks like it's been poured onto her. After a few steps, she's engulfed by the crowd. Oh well, at least my New Year's kiss streak is intact. I wish I'd gotten her name.

The Devil Birds team owners take the stage—gorgeous witch and casino owner Teagan Penhall, seagull shifter Jake Whitman, and cougar shifter Coach Liam Morgan.

Teagan takes the microphone and waits for the crowd to quiet down. She has a way of commanding attention. I don't know if it's her witchy powers or her stunning beauty as she stands regally in her sexy glittery black dress, but soon the crowd is quiet, waiting to hear what she has to say.

"Thank you all for welcoming in the new year with us! I hope you've had a wonderful time tonight. Please join me in wishing the Devil Birds a successful second half of the season and a deep playoff run." She raises her champagne flute, and the room follows suit. "Go Devil Birds!"

Cheers rise throughout the room. "Go Birds!" And mostly imitation seagull cries fill the air. I know there's at least one seagull shifter here.

Next, Coach takes the microphone. "Happy New Year, everyone. Before you go back to celebrating, we have one more thing to do. Where's Carter?" He searches the crowd until he finds me. "There you are." He gestures with his head. "Come on up here."

What's going on? I make my way through the crowd and join Coach on the stage. He's smiling and waving to the crowd, but I'm standing there, confused.

"You're our first-line center and my future brother-in-law," he says. There are some hoots and hollers from the crowd, which he silences with a wave of his hand. "You showed us your moves on the dance floor tonight." Now there are cheers, and he yells through them. "So I dare you to dance! You've been chosen to compete in the upcoming season of *Celebrity Dance Dare- Shifter Edition!*"

Confusion turns to shock, and as I scan the crowd, my eyes widen, probably to the size of the hockey pucks I shoot in the net every chance I get. I'm not sure who or what I'm looking for. A camera crew joins us on stage. Oh god, they're filming this?

Coach slaps me on the back to shake me out of my daze. "Meet your partner, Sophie Mackenzie!"

My beautiful blonde midnight kiss walks across the stage, smiling and waving. I'm still in shock, gaping like an idiot. What the hell is going on here?

"Trevor," she says warmly, an Irish lilt giving her voice a musical tone like tinkling bells. She takes my hands in hers, acting like our tongues weren't doing the tango ten minutes ago. "It's so nice to meet you! I hope you have your dancing shoes laced up because together we're going to win the Platinum Paw! Are you with me?"

"You're my partner?" I ask. "How are we going to train with me playing?" I'm a professional hockey player. That's my focus, not two-stepping on TV, trying to win a stupid trophy. *Platinum Paw.* Spare me. Sounds like a prosthetic for a poodle.

Sophie nods, smiling like she's in a toothpaste commercial. It's a beautiful smile, but the daggers she's shooting at me with her eyes contradict it.

"We'll go over the details later," Coach says before smiling at the crowd again. "The Devil Birds are such a big, happy family that even your dance partner is part of it. Sophie is your linemate Declan Mackenzie's sister! Mac, come on up!"

Teagan murmurs something the mic doesn't pick up. But based on the fact that Mac's nowhere to be seen, it must have to do with him.

Coach nods and faces the crowd again, glossing over my missing linemate. "You'll train together and compete on national television to bring home that Platinum Paw trophy. We gotta start filling our trophy case at The Nest! Show 'em how it's done!"

Sophie steps forward like she's going to kiss my cheek, so I bend down to make it easier for her.

"Stop standing there like a flipping idiot and smile! You look like someone put Vaseline in your dance belt," she hisses in my ear as she pretends to kiss my cheek. "You're my ticket to getting a permanent pro spot on the show. You will *not* screw this up for me. Now smile, damn it!"

I shudder. No one wants petroleum jelly sliming up their twig and berries. This little hellion would probably do that to me. I knew Mac had a younger sister, but he never mentioned she was a dancer. Or that she's gorgeous. All he's shared is that she's a wolf shifter like him, from their father's side of the family. She's a witch, too, thanks to their mother. He's one of my roommates, renting a room above the converted barn I have on my family's property. He's a quiet man, even-tempered. His sister, not so much.

"Okay," I say. "Fine, Soph."

"My name is Sophie, *Travis*."

"How about I just call you princess?"

"Okay, arsehole."

Stifling a bark of laughter, I straighten to my full height. I break out my cheer smile, that fake curve of the lips I used for years as a cheerleader. I was expected to smile and make everything look effortless while holding a grown woman over my head with one arm. She'd be fifteen feet in the air, giving the same fake smile and praying I didn't drop her. And I'd be praying the same thing, hoping she wouldn't break an arm or crack her head open.

Sophie's got the same fake smile now, probably hoping I don't break whatever this is happening around us, and just like I did during cheer, after delivering my partner safely back to the ground after a stunt, I hold my hand up and wave at the cheering crowd.

1

TREVOR

I love being in the rink with my teammates. The scrape of blades on ice and the thwack of sticks against the puck have a rhythm that I feel in my blood. It's almost musical. The plays are like a choreographed dance we need to practice if we want to perform them correctly. Dancing with the puck on the end of my stick is the only waltz I want to do. The power play is my paso doble. And the penalty kill is the bane of my existence. For some reason, we aren't gelling on it lately, and we need to work it out. We don't incur a lot of penalties. We're a pretty disciplined team. But even only one failed PK per game can result in the game-winning goal for the opposing team and the loss of our place in the league standings.

Defenseman Stone Waller practices the power play this round, stripping the puck from our teammate playing offense on the line. Stone passes it to me, and I take off down the ice toward my opponent's goal. As much as we want to stop being scored on during penalty kills, we want to make shorthanded goals if at all possible. I pass the puck to another teammate, and it sails right past him. He was two strides behind where he should've been. When Coach blows the whistle, I slam my stick against the ice in frustration and skate to the bench for some water. My regular linemate, Sophie's brother Mac, is sitting there with a cast on his hand. He broke it punching a wall when his girlfriend's mother wouldn't let him see her. His girlfriend, Randi, is my best friend from college, and I understand he's in love and her mother's a bitch, but he *broke his hand* because he was heartbroken. He's not going to be able to play for a few weeks, meaning he'll miss the PHL's first All-Star Game. He let his emotions screw up his hockey career.

"He'll get it," Mac says in his Scottish-Irish brogue. "Crosby's a hard-working player. He'll keep at it. You'll be okay."

"Only if we can get enough reps in." I look up at the scoreboard to check the clock and sigh. I'm out of time. "Hard to get the reps in if I'm not here. I need to go practice with your sister."

If I had my way, I'd blow off this first dance practice, but Coach knows the schedule and is looking at me with a raised brow. Damn it, time to go. With a curt nod to Coach, I leave the ice and change in the locker room.

I head to the Devil's Den Theater, where Sophie and I are practicing. They have a stage and a dance studio space. We'll practice for two hours before I go back to the rink to watch video before tonight's game. It's a weird week—a home game and then flying down to Florida for the PHL All-Star Game, and somewhere in all of that, we need to practice for our first dance. This is going to be a routine with rules. It's not going to be fun and freedom.

"Good morning!" Sophie calls out as I approach the stage. She's in leggings and a fitted T-shirt. I'm in a T-shirt and joggers.

"Hey," I say. "How are you?"

She shrugs. "All right. Eager to dance. If I'm dancing, then I can forget about everything else for a while."

I get that, it's how I feel on the ice. "Okay, let's do this. What's our first dance?"

"Cha-cha." She cocks her head. "Have you ever danced it?"

"Nope." I watched some videos online, but I don't know if that will win me points or not.

"I'll text you some links if you want to get an idea of what to expect. It's a Latin dance that originated in Cuba in the 1950s. It's sharp hip and leg action and footwork. Here comes the camera person. They'll have you walk back in, and we'll have this conversation again. If we can give them a bit of friction, that will make it more interesting."

I'd like to give her some friction, but not on camera. I haven't been able to forget our midnight kiss, no matter how hard I've tried. Speaking of hard, my dick wants to point north anytime we're in the same room. I try to keep my focus where it needs to be, but it always strays to her.

A tall, lanky man with a mop of yellow hair and a camera perched on his shoulder walks toward us with an easy grin. "Good morning! I'm Nigel, one of your camerapeople. Your producer, Nancy, will be here in a moment."

"Hi, Nigel." I hold out my hand to shake.

Sophie shakes his hand next. "Hey, Nige, they shipped you over too?"

"Yeah, there's a few of us from the mother ship here. Not just you."

"Mother ship?" I ask.

"That's what we call the UK version of *Celebrity Dance Dare*," Nigel says. "That was the original show, and all the others are spin-offs from that. And for Sophie, with her mother being one of the judges, we mean *mother* ship."

A woman rushes in, and it looks so natural that I think rushing is her normal gear. She must be the producer. Her black pencil skirt and tightly tucked white blouse scream no-nonsense business. Her hair is cut in a severe black bob, emphasizing her pointy little chin. No smile graces her razor-thin lips, but what really catches me off guard is something ugly in her eyes when she looks at Sophie.

"Oh good, you're here," she says, sounding anything but happy.

"Yes, Sophie's mother. How *fortunate* she is to have that connection."
Okay, whatever this woman's name is, she will forever be Bitchy
McBitchface to me. The way she emphasized the word *fortunate*, it's
clear she meant the only way Sophie had a spot on the show was
because of her mother.

Sophie sucks in her breath and slowly exhales. That bitch hurt
her, and Sophie's doing her best not to show it. I don't need it spelled
out for me. I hear whispers that I got my spot on the team because
the coach is engaged to my sister. I know I must work twice as hard
to prove I earned my spot and deserve to be on the ice. It seems
Sophie knows exactly what that's like.

"Hello, Nancy," Sophie says.

The way she keeps her voice neutral is amazing. In the few days
we've known each other I've heard her scream like a banshee, I've
seen her be snarky. This is the first time I've seen her hold her anger.

"We only have Trevor for an hour and a half before he has to go
do hockey things, so what do you want us to do first?"

"Well, we already have the footage of you meeting at the
announcement. Let's have you tell him about the dance," Nancy says.
"Have you done any choreography yet?"

"I've started on it," Sophie says. "I want to discuss it with
Trevor."

"It's your job to tell him what to do," the bitch says. "You're the
pro. Act like it."

Before I spout off, Sophie jumps in. "Nancy, I know my job.
Trevor is my *partner*. He's allowed to have thoughts and input."

Ooh, I like it when Sophie uses her snark for good.

"That's not how Ian does it."

What is up with this woman? How is this professional behavior?

Sophie shifts her weight and puts a hand on her hip. "Well, I'm
not my brother."

Is it wrong I find this display of sass sexy?

"Yeah, you're not. He wins." Nancy gives that 'so there' sniff and
looks down her nose at Sophie from her greater height. She's a good

six inches taller, and she's trying to use that as an intimidation tactic. Sophie refuses to be intimidated. This is fun to watch.

"Yeah, he does. Those that can, dance. Those that can't, produce." Sophie gives her own 'so there' face right back.

I realize Nigel is surreptitiously recording the exchange on his phone. I don't know what he's going to do with it, but the wink he gives me when he realizes I notice what he's doing is giving me hope he isn't going to use it against Sophie.

"Okay," I say. "Let's get started. Sophie, tell me what our dance is. I trust you. I'll follow your lead and make you a winner."

She holds up her hand for a high five. She's short, so it's really a mid-five for me, but I appreciate the sentiment. "Make *us* winners."

I like how she says us. I know she doesn't mean it the way my brain does. This is our first rehearsal. We've known each other less than a week, and other than that kiss on New Year's, nothing has happened between us. There isn't an us. That's okay. Nigel is ready with his camera, and Nancy nods for us to start talking.

"So, our first routine is a cha-cha," Sophie says.

"That's a Latin dance from Cuba with sharp hip and leg action and footwork, right?" I ask with a wink.

The way she pops a dimple while trying to hold back a smile is adorable.

"How much experience do you have with choreography?" she asks. I shrug. "I'm used to counts and memorizing choreo from cheerleading, but there aren't tempo changes the same way there are in dance. When I dance, it's usually contemporary, so there's choreography but not the same rules."

Nancy stands next to Nigel, tapping her toe, lips pursed. I hope she's just here for this first rehearsal and leaves us alone most of the time after this.

"You were a cheerleader?" Nancy asks. "Like with pom-poms?" The disdain she feels is evident. I don't know if she's anti-pom-pom, anti-male cheerleaders, or anti-people in general.

Next to me, Sophie stiffens. I'm so used to the question it doesn't bother me, but I appreciate Sophie's reaction.

"No pom-poms," I tell her. "I was the muscle. Lifting, throwing, tumbling."

"Can I continue?" Sophie asks. It takes a lot of effort, but I hold back the chuckle that's trying to escape.

Nancy flutters her hand like she's granting royal permission. I can't stand this woman, and I don't want to work with her. I need to go over my contract again. An advantage of my law degree is I know my way around a contract. I don't have a say in my partner, but I think I can request a different producer.

After taking a deep breath, Sophie gives a bright smile that's as fake as Nancy's tan and starts her spiel.

"The cha-cha is all about rhythm, energy, and having a great time on the dance floor. Yes, it has that signature hip action. As we move, let your hips sway a bit." She demonstrates, and I'm transfixed by the metronomic motion of her hips. When she keeps talking, I force myself to pay attention to her words and not just her body's hypnotizing sway.

"It's like a little side-to-side movement that adds flair and fun to the dance. Feel the music and let your body respond to the beat."

Oh, my body is responding, all right. The way her eyes widen slightly makes me wonder if her witch powers include mind reading. They certainly include making me lose focus.

"Um..." Sophie looks like she's trying to remember what she was going to say. "The cha-cha is all about having fun and enjoying the music. It'll take practice and working together, but I'm confident you're going to get it. We've got this."

"We do," I say, giving her a hug. Once I have my arms around her, I decide to go for it and lift her up and spin with her. I hear her giggle for the first time, and after the craziness we've gone through the past couple of days, it's the most beautiful sound I've heard this year.

There's about twenty minutes before I need to get to The Nest. We listen to our music. It's a fast-paced song from the early 90s. If my parents ever went to a club, they would've danced to it. Not that I can picture them ever being somewhere more exciting than the library on a Saturday night.

"Are you going to the Devil Birds game tonight?" I ask Sophie. She nods.

"I'll be there too," Nigel says. "I want to get some background video we can use for packages."

Nancy gives a huff. "I'll be going back to New York. Nigel will send me dailies, and I'll be communicating with Sophie to make sure you're on track. The premiere is in two weeks. Your Thursdays will be dress rehearsal and then the live show. You'll be required to travel to New York for media. It's been cleared with your coaches."

"The show goes seven weeks maximum, right?" I glance at Sophie.

"Yeah," she confirms.

That'll take us to the start of playoffs for the Dickinson Cup. I want my name to be among the first engraved on it. I can't let competing for a Platinum Paw trophy keep me from winning the trophy that's truly important. Surely we can prove Sophie deserves a permanent spot, even if we don't make it all the way to the finals. I'm not risking my team's success and the hard work we've done all season so I can wear some rhinestones and shimmy for two months.

I don't know if anyone else knows the PHL's schedule well enough to realize the conflict. My parents may not have been affectionate, but they're certainly smart, and one of the things they taught me was to pick my battles. No reason to cause waves now when there's a strong chance we won't even make the finals.

"Okay, see you guys at the game," I say to Nigel. "I'm sure our team social media manager, Daphne, has a seat saved for you both. We'll get the footage you need, Nige. Nancy, I hope you have a safe trip back to New York."

I purposely don't say that it was nice to meet her or hope to see her again soon. Another thing my parents taught me was not to lie.

Sophie is doing some steps in front of the mirror, muttering corrections to herself. Her eyes, normally a clear blue, are a stormier color. Is she sad? Mad?

"Are you okay?" I ask, standing just behind her and looking at our reflections in the mirror.

"Fine," she says. "After all that's happened..." She swallows hard and squares her shoulders, still not meeting my eyes in the mirror. "I'm fine."

I think she's reassuring herself as much as she's reassuring me. How can she be fine after everything that happened over the last three days? Discovering her best friend's mother had been drugging her with a witch's brew of a tea for over a decade? Falling out with almost everyone close to her?

Randi's mother, Doreen, is a nasty, evil woman who used her knowledge as a witch to create a blend of tea leaves and other herbs to make the person drinking the tea susceptible to suggestion. She'd send "I don't care about you" packages to Randi while she was at boarding school in order to keep Randi's unknown powers as a witch suppressed because she was jealous of her. She supplied Sophie too and filled her mind with lies and jealousy to drive a wedge between Sophie and Randi. I can imagine it affected other relationships in her life throughout the years, too. I know it strained the one with her mother, Nora.

If all that had happened to me, I'd have holed myself up in a cave somewhere until I'd figured it all out. Not Sophie. Apparently she doesn't run. She's strong.

But still...I don't want to leave her when she obviously has stuff on her mind.

I have to though. I need to get back to The Nest to watch video and get notes for tonight's game. I'm attracted to Sophie, and I want to comfort her, but I'm not here for that. I'm only here to dance with her. Correction—I'm only here to play hockey.

"Okay," I say, zipping up my Devil Birds fleece that will ward off the freezing wind blowing off the Atlantic on my walk back from Devil's Den to The Nest. "See you later."

She nods. "Aye."

Her back is still to me and her eyes are avoiding mine in the mirror. Fine. Whatever. I glance back as I exit...and meet Sophie's eyes in the mirror. Just for a moment, before she looks away, but the connection is there. Whether we acknowledge it or not.

2

SOPHIE

THIS IS MY FIRST TIME ATTENDING AN ICE HOCKEY MATCH. GAME? I'M NOT exactly sure what they call it. I'm uncertain how Dec ended up here. I know he'd skate on the loch with Miranda when we were kids but I didn't think that would become this. Maybe he played while he was attending university in New York. My family is into horses. We're Irish and Scottish, we'd play rugby, maybe shinty if we were doing stuff with sticks. Not ice hockey.

Our parents are here, too. Daphne, the team's social media manager who's married to the coach's cousin, has given us all Devil Birds shirts to wear. Ma and Dad have sweatshirts with Mackenzie on the nameplate and Dec's number 80 on it. I have a generic team sweatshirt since I'll be attending a bunch of games as Trevor's dance partner as well as Dec's sister. Everyone goes by last names, so Declan is Mac and Trevor is Carter. It's confusing as hell. Going by Mac at home would never work with so many Mackenzies around.

I wish Declan was playing tonight. I know I'll have other chances to see him play once his hand is healed, but I don't know when our parents will get to see him play live. Now that I'm emerging from the tea fog, I can see just how screwed up my actions were over the last few weeks. Dec smashes his hand into a wall, and I blame Miranda because she broke up with him? Guilt twists in my gut. I can't understand how I could've ever thought that. Dec's responsible for his own shitty actions, not her. I shouldn't blame myself for my actions while drugged, but I can't help it. I know I was a bitch to Miranda because she broke up with Declan, a choice she'd made while under the influence of the tea too. And even if she had really wanted to break up with him, he should respect that choice, not choose violence. I should have accepted that choice. It's a mess, and I can't help but feel some guilt, even though I know the tea and Miranda's mum caused all the trouble. I rub at my temples, where a headache has started pounding.

Dec is watching the game with us from the owner's box. He's toward the back, so he isn't as easily seen by the crowd. I understand not wanting to be gawked at by spectators. It's been announced he's injured and will miss the All-Star Game with a broken hand, but obviously how he broke it wasn't disclosed.

Team owners Teagan Penhall and Jake Whitman are in the box. So are Daphne, the coach's fiancée Mallory, the team captain's girlfriend Kendall, and some other folks I was introduced to but can't quite remember details about. It's not crowded, but it's not completely private either. That's fine by me. No questions about the craziness from the past few days with Miranda and her family or feelings or anything else I want to avoid. Nigel is wandering around with Daphne's husband, Logan, the Devil Birds' team photographer.

"You started rehearsing today?" Ma asks as we watch the players take the ice for practice. Everyone has their helmets on, but I can pick out Trevor by the way he moves even before I see the Carter and number 24 on the back of his gray-and-blue jersey. I know he's a wolf shifter like me, but he's smooth and almost graceful—like a powerful jungle cat stalking his prey. If a disk of hard rubber could be considered prey. I guess it's a good thing I'm a dancer and not a writer.

"Yeah, just the meeting with Nigel and Nancy..."

Ma makes an ew face. "You got Nancy? She's the worst. No one wants to work with her. That's how she ended up on the shifter show."

I don't think Ma realizes she essentially called the US shifter edition of *Celebrity Dance Dare* the dumping grounds of the CDD world. Is that how I ended up on it? I'm not good enough for the UK or Irish versions, not even the Irish shifter *Celebrity Dance Dare*, so I got shipped off here?

"Yes," I say, "but she went back to New York, and we have Nigel as our cameraperson. He's lovely."

Ma nods. "Nigel is lovely. One of the best camerapeople in the whole franchise. I guess he's making up for Nancy."

That's like saying a cupcake can make up for the bubonic plague, but sure.

"What's your first dance? Oh, thanks." Ma accepts the drink Dad hands her as he sits next to her.

I guess I can die of thirst. There's a bar at the back of the box so I'll grab something myself, but it would've been nice to have been thought of. Whatever. I'm used to it.

"Cha-cha. He's used to counts and choreo but for cheerleading. I don't know if he can be fluid with choreography. But he can certainly dance. I just don't know if he can move with that freedom while following steps." I cock my head, hoping I'm making sense. "Do you know what I mean?"

Ma nods. "Absolutely. That happens a lot. Sometimes it's the folks that don't have a dance background at all that do the best. They're a blank slate, so we don't have to retrain them or undo what they're used to. Does he want to do the show?"

I shake my head. "I don't think so. It was sprung on him. You know it's a promo for the team and the league. But he's being a good sport about it, and I think he's going to try his best. Can't ask for more than that."

Dad leans forward. "How are you going to balance practice and hockey? Are you traveling with the team?"

"I am. We have a practice space at Devil's Den. He has a dance studio in the barn they all live in. We'll work it out. We only need to be in New York one day each week for the live shows, and the way the schedule is, there aren't games on live show days, but who knows if there will be any press commitments that screw things up. If he has to miss a lot of games, he's going to resist."

"Well, he'll just have to deal with it," Dad says. "My little girl wants to win the Platinum Paw."

He reaches across Ma's lap to pat my hand. I have to swallow a couple of times to work the lump back down my throat. I know Dad loves me, but it's been forever since he's called me his little girl. I was always grumpy that Miranda was included in everything when we were girls, but considering how screwed up her childhood was, I'm so grateful we were loved and protected by my parents. Dad always made sure we were safe. Of course, as a child, I didn't have the maturity to see how valuable that was. Okay, I didn't have the maturity four days ago either, but I'm growing up.

The Devil Birds are playing some Sasquatch team from out west. Their mascot is a big hairy thing. Honestly, I'm not sure it's someone in a costume. It may just be a Bigfoot shifter fan. I'm surprised they make jerseys and jeans that big. I think the sassy seagull the Devil Birds use is cuter. Cute may not be the right word. Like all seagulls, Shifty the Seagull, also known as Shitty, has an asshole attitude. If I saw him outside with a cigarette, I wouldn't be surprised. His beak has a slight hook to it, like it's been punched a time or two. But it's someone in a seagull costume, not a real seagull shifter.

It's not the spectators or mascots that are capturing my attention though—it's Trevor. His helmet covers his deep brown hair with chestnut tones. The face shield probably does nothing to hide the intense focus he gets in his hazel eyes when he's in the zone. I saw it briefly when we were dancing earlier today. I appreciate the focus, but unlike hockey, you can't show how hard you're thinking when you're dancing.

The game starts, and it's exhilarating to watch him. He fights for the puck in the opening face-off with a steely determination I can't help but admire. He goes after what he wants. I just hope winning *Celebrity Dance Dare* is something he wants enough. He's agile and fearless. Trevor's not the biggest man on the ice or even the biggest man on his team, but my eyes are drawn to him every time he's out there. If he can bring that kind of magnetism to the dance floor, we'll be hard to beat.

He's graceful, too, the way he weaves in and out of the paths of the opposing players, trying to take the puck away from him. The way he glides across the ice is almost balletic. You can see how hard some of the other players work to propel themselves along the ice—when they have to change direction, it's like turning a barge. Trevor zips along and covers the ice as effortlessly as water running downhill. He flows. How he controls not only his body but a however-many-meters-long stick and the puck is beautiful to watch. I need to figure out a way to work hockey into one of our dances.

No matter how hard he works, he can't get the puck in the net though. It's like he's out of sync with one of his linemates. I wonder if he's Dec's replacement? I know what it's like to have to adjust choreography to dance with a new partner and adapt to their hand not being where you're used to finding it and tweaking the timing. Eventually, you get it, but until you do, it's frustrating. That's what seems to be going on here. Multiple times Trevor passes the puck to his winger—I had to look that word up—and the player is a step or two too far back; he can't reach the puck with his stick. It looks like he's shorter than Dec and they aren't accounting for how Dec's giant strides affect the timing. If Trevor holds the puck for another second or two before passing, the other player will be in position. I can see Trevor's annoyance in the set of his shoulders, even underneath the pads he wears as he leaves the ice after the scoreless first period.

"Watch Shifty," Mallory says from the seat next to me, nudging me with her elbow. Miranda left before the period ended to go to the locker room. As assistant to the team's coach, I guess Miranda's job calls for her to be with him in the locker room during intermission to take notes or whatever. Dec is on his phone sending texts.

I nod and find the mascot in the aisle by the seats below our box. He bends forward, aiming his backside at the crowd. Suddenly, there's a pop, and a shower of white shoots out. There's an excited shout and a teenage girl holds up a T-shirt.

"Good lord! Did he just shoot that out of his arse?" I don't mean to say it out loud, but I clearly do because Teagan laughs.

"Yeah, his costume has an ASS Cannon built in," Teagan says with pride. She stands at the front of the box, near our seats. "Air Supplied Souvenir Cannon. It's a specially designed T-shirt cannon built into the costume. First of its kind."

I shake my head. "It's glorious."

The white glitter confetti is supposed to be like seagull shit. The way it gets all over the place is true to life. It's incredible.

Shifty steals a few fries from a Sasquatch fan and moves on. Yep, true to life.

"Have you and Carter started practicing yet?" Teagan asks.

Mallory's grin turns mischievous. "Please make him wear sequins and feathers. And he's a huge fan of the song 'Copacabana.' Loves it." She's not only engaged to the Devil Birds' coach, she's Trevor's sister, and she's clearly hoping to use me to torment him.

I love torturing my brothers, too, and I return her grin. "Pink? Or purple?"

She tilts her head and taps her lips with a forefinger in consideration. Her engagement ring sparkles in the lights of the arena. "Hmm...I'm not evil. How about turquoise? Blue is his favorite color."

I didn't know that. Now I do. And for some reason, I like knowing.

I turn back to Teagan. "I told him what our first dance is and the music. We started with some of the basic steps today."

"Oh." Mallory glances down at the ice. Both teams are back, and the next period is about to start. "Well, he's always been stubborn, so if he wants to do this, there will be no stopping him."

As the second period opens, Trevor is laser-focused on the spot where the ref will drop the puck between him and the opposing player in the face-off circle. With lightning-fast reflexes, he takes control of the puck the moment it touches the ice surface and flicks it back to his teammates. They advance like a battalion on the battle-field as they approach the opposing goal. It's like a game of keep-away, and following the location of the puck is tricky. Daphne's tip is to follow the people more than the puck specifically. It helps. Of course, my eyes are fixed on Trevor whenever he's on the ice. I can't look away. He's usually the one with the puck anyway. This period, it's like Trevor and his winger are sharing a brain. The winger is in the right spot time and again to receive Trevor's passes. He's able to direct the puck back to Trevor so he can put it in the net. Trevor does this move Daphne tells me is called a "one-timer" where he plants himself on the ice, takes a full backswing, and propels the puck to the net like it was shot from a cannon.

Even in full uniform, you can see the tension of his muscles and the power of his movements. Trevor is so focused I don't think he's aware of the crowd shouting his name or even of the other team. If I was ever the subject of his focus like that, I think I'd erupt in flames. Even our spur-of-the-moment New Year's kiss, where I had a frac-tion of his attention, is something I can't forget. I know I shouldn't have kissed him at all because I knew we'd be working together as dance partners and it would be a possible complication, but I couldn't resist. There are more handsome men out there, some I've even been with. But none of them have the magnetism Trevor does. Maybe it's because he's a wolf shifter, and my wolf is reacting to him on a primal level. Maybe it's all just biology. Or maybe there's some-thing more. Doesn't matter. There can't be anything outside of a professional partnership between us. I want that trophy. That's all that matters.

Trevor's got all his attention on the opposing goal, and when he shoots the puck past the goalie, it takes him a beat to react to his teammates hugging him. But his focus doesn't seem to be on them.

He's looking up in the stands. At me. I'm with the thousands of other fans standing and cheering, but his gaze zeros in on me like a heat-seeking missile. I can't look away.

It's not always the best dancer that wins shows like *Celebrity Dance Dare*. Sometimes it's the contestant who rallies the audience behind them and does the best job entertaining. The judges are paying attention to the steps, but the audience is all about the feelings. I'm betting he's going to be great at stirring feelings. He's stirring some in me.

The Devil Birds beat the Sasquatch thanks to Trevor's goals. Tomorrow, we leave for the All-Star Game in Florida. The Devil Birds players and their families will travel on their private plane and I'm included in the entourage. I'm hoping it will give me a chance to talk to Miranda and clear the air. I miss my best friend. I miss *being* a best friend. I go back across the Boardwalk to the hotel with my parents and hug them outside of my room. They're flying back home tomorrow. They could've gone to Florida to be with me, but I guess that didn't occur to them.

They came here for Miranda. She's doing better now and going to the All-Star Game with the team, so there's no reason for them to stay, especially since Dec won't be playing. It must be so hard to watch your teammates compete and succeed without you. I know I'd hate to be sidelined by an injury, especially if it's my own stupidity that caused it. It's ridiculous that he gave up being in the spotlight because of a broken heart. No way am I ever letting love get in the way of my goals. I'm not stupid enough to let love ruin my chances at success and keep me out of the spotlight.

I ride to the airport with some of the player families and other VIPs that are flying down to Florida on the team plane. The players and staff, including Miranda, will meet us at the airport since they're coming from their homes.

As I climb the steps onto the plane, I spot Miranda toward the back. There's an empty seat next to her, and she's chatting with a flight attendant.

"Okay if I sit here?" I ask, resting my hand on the back of the empty seat.

She gives me a soft smile. "Yeah, that would be great."

I whoosh out a breath, hoping it expels the flock of butterflies fluttering in my tummy, and flash a smile at the flight attendant, who steps away to make room for me. I take the seat, stashing my bag under Carter's seat in front of me.

"Good afternoon, miss. I'm Stella. Would you like something to drink after takeoff?"

"Hi, Stella, I'm Sophie." I hold out my hand for Stella to shake.

Stella's smile widens. "Are you Declan's sister?"

"I am," I say, arching my eyebrows. "Is it the accent?"

"No, you have the same color eyes."

"Oh." I wonder if she has a thing for Declan. Hopefully, she's not like Doreen and won't drug Miranda.

"What are you drinking?" I ask Miranda.

"Hot cocoa with whipped cream, but Stella makes wonderful tea."

The thought of tea makes me shudder.

"I'll have cocoa too, please, with whipped cream?"

Stella smiles and says she'll bring our cocoa after we are airborne.

Miranda and I settle in but don't converse other than basic questions like if I enjoyed the game and how entertaining the Shifty mascot is. She shows me a video from when he was first introduced to the public and there was a speaker malfunction, so it sounded like the little girl announcing his name said Shitty instead of Shifty. Thinking back to the glitter-poop cannon built into his suit, I can see they're leaning into that identity. It's hilarious.

Takeoff is uneventful, and once we're at altitude, Stella brings us our hot cocoas and a plate of snickerdoodles to share. Snickerdoodles are my weakness, and I can't resist closing my eyes as I chew. She heated the cookies, and I savor the cinnamon and sugar melting on my tongue. I feel Miranda's eyes on me, so I open mine and grin at her.

"Remember all those times we'd *help* Siobhan with the baking, and she'd give us a treat?" I say, making air quotes when I say "help." We were a hindrance, but our family's cook was a sweetheart who baked like a dream. She's retired now, with a passel of grandkids she lives to spoil.

Miranda sighs. "I loved spending time with you doing that." She turns in her seat to face me. Uh-oh, this is it.

"Soph, what happened? We were such great friends, but lately, it feels like you're mad at me. If I offended or hurt you, I don't know why or how. I love you and want to make up for whatever I did."

Tears flood my eyes, and I swallow hard and maneuver to rest my back against the armrest and face Miranda. This needs to be done face-to-face. Here we go. Truth time.

"Oh, Miranda, I'm sorry. You did nothing wrong. I wish I could blame everything on your narcissistic psychopath of a mother, but part of it was, I was jealous of you."

Her jaw drops. I guess that never occurred to her. Of course not, because she's a good person. She reaches out and takes my clammy hand, and I cringe at my sweaty palm, but it doesn't seem to faze her.

"Jealous of me? Why? You're beautiful and talented. You have a wonderful family that loves you." She gives my hand a gentle squeeze. "Sophie, you have everything I've ever wanted."

I squeeze her fingers. "I know I'm blessed, and I'm grateful for that. But I'm selfish. Growing up, everyone loved you. You were this perfect little girl that everyone adored. I'm pretty sure you're my mother's favorite child."

Miranda giggles like that's absurd.

"I'm not kidding. The two of you just get each other in a way that she and I don't. I don't know if we're too similar or too different or a bit of both, but it can be difficult." I shrug. "I always wanted her attention, and as her only daughter, I felt it was my right. But she was focused on you a lot, and I was jealous. Knowing what we know now, and with whatever smidgeon of wisdom adulthood has given me, I'm so grateful she was there for you. But sometimes I wanted it to be just me and her, and it wasn't, because you were included." I can't hold back the tears now streaming down my cheeks. "I'm so sorry, Miranda."

She squeezes my hand gently, and I feel it around my heart. "Sophie, that's understandable. We were children and, of course you wanted your mother's attention and to be separate from your brothers. I'm sorry I intruded. Things should've been different for both of us."

I wipe my nose with the napkin Stella gave me with the cocoa and give a watery laugh.

"I hate calling her your mother, so I'm calling her Doreen from now on. Doreen recognized how I felt and used that to drive a wedge between me and you. Between me and my family, too. I can see now how she manipulated me. How she used that damn tea."

"It's scary," Miranda says, grabbing her own napkin to wipe her eyes.

It's terrifying thinking how Doreen could have poisoned either of us and the horrible situations she could have put Miranda in. Thank goodness Miranda was parked in all those boarding schools, considering what could've happened if she lived with that viper.

"I'll get you tissues," Stella says, checking in on us. I guess our faces tell the tale.

"I'm sorry too, Sophie. We were both victims. Can we put that behind us and just start again? I love you, and you've been like the sister I've always wanted. I don't want what happened to come between us."

Stella returns with the tissues, and we thank her. After we both take a moment to wipe our faces—I am so grateful for waterproof mascara—and declare each other beautiful, we each grab a cookie and settle in our seats.

I grin. "I want to move forward in our friendship and be close again. I would love to have you as a sister." I wiggle my eyebrows. "Or a sister-in-law."

Miranda blinks rapidly. Shit. I didn't mean to make her cry. I'm trying to make things better, not tear us apart again. I lean toward her, and I hope she can tell I'm speaking from the heart.

"Declan loves you. He wasn't under any spells or the influence of potions or anything."

"I asked him to give me space." She speaks softly to her hands, neatly folded across the cookie in her lap.

"I caught that." I scratch the back of my neck, unsure what to say next. But there's really only one thing to say. "His heart has always been true, and it's always been yours. He's going to give you space because you asked him to. The next move is yours. If you want him, tell him." I take a deep breath because I'm afraid this next bit is going to put a wall between us again, but I need to say it.

"But please, be sure. It would be kinder to break his heart now than to lead him on and break it later."

Miranda nods, swallowing.

"To moving forward," I say, hoping we can truly do that.

"To moving forward," Miranda echoes, lifting her mug of no-longer-hot cocoa to clink it against mine.

We spend the rest of the flight to Florida gossiping and giggling. This is how it always should've been between us. I hope, from now on, it always will be.

3
TREVOR

THE WEATHER IS BEAUTIFUL IN FLORIDA. MY PARENTS LIVE IN ORLANDO, AND with the warm sunshine, I understand the appeal, but I'm a fan of having four seasons. They're semi-retired from their careers as a patent attorney—Dad—and a chemical engineer—Mom. They're both type A personalities, hence being only *semi*-retired.

Our bus pulls up in front of the hotel we're at for the next few days. It's a Clardmore. We usually stay at one of their properties whenever possible—they're a shifter-owned company. The shifters that own them? Sophie's family. It's right next door to the Florida Storm Chasers' arena. The Chasers aren't a shifter hockey team. They're part of the regular pro human hockey league. The PHL doesn't have a team in Florida, so it was chosen as neutral ground— and because people want to come to Florida in January. In future years, the All-Star Game will be held in the arena of whatever team wins the Dickinson Cup the prior season. So, I'm betting next year's game will be in Atlantic City, and I'm pretty sure only polar bear shifters like Bedard will hit the beach then.

Sophie and Randi are sitting on the opposite side of the bus, and they're leaning over to peer at the hotel through my window.

"Did you know about this?" Randi asks Sophie.

Sophie shakes her head and looks at Randi like she's crazy. "No, I have nothing to do with the hotels and I'm not consulted on Devil Birds travel plans." With a grin, she adds, "At least we know the beds will be comfy."

"True. And you can probably get me a free dessert or something at dinner."

Sophie giggles. "Way to dream big, Miranda. I don't know if Declan's going to be able to afford you."

"Who's saying I won't be keeping him in the style he's accustomed to? I have a trust from my grandmother that'll help make my future more comfortable."

"Randi, you've already started spending that trust fund. And it'll take some work before you're comfortable," I say with a wink. She's trying to purchase a farm that's for sale across the street from me.

"What are you doing?" Sophie asks.

"I can't say anything yet because nothing is definite. As soon as I can discuss it, you'll be one of the first to know. I promise." Miranda's gray eyes are earnest as she makes her vow. Her fingers are crossed, but I can tell by her expression it's in hopefulness for whatever she has in the works. Miranda isn't the deceitful type. Never has been.

We file into the hotel lobby, and I get my room assignment from Daphne. We're all on the same floor, which is convenient from an organization standpoint, but makes it tricky to hook up with anyone. No one wants to be caught doing the walk of shame in yesterday's clothes by your teammate's granny.

The atmosphere at the hotel and in the arena is incredible. There are meet and greets with the players where fans get to have items signed and their pictures taken. The different teams have parties for their fans and there are fun skill challenges for the players.

A few hours later, we're all suited up and about to start the skills competition. I love the jerseys—The Atlantic Conference were given gray jerseys, Central Conference has red, and Western Conference is white. The crowd erupts with cheers and even some boos as we skate around the ice. The stands are a rainbow of jerseys from all the different teams represented in the skills competitions. Even though we're in Florida, the chill of the rink has folks bundled up in hoodies. I spot Sophie and Randi and skate over to the bench closest to them. I wave Sophie over, and she joins me at the glass.

Between raising my voice and lip reading, I'm able to talk to her. "I got jerseys for you and Randi. One is a spare of mine, and the other is one of Mac's. They had already made up his jerseys before he was injured and still had them in the locker room. I asked if I could have them for his sister and girlfriend and they gave them to me. I don't know if Randi wants to wear his. That's why I picked one of each—you can decide how to divvy it up. Since you're my dance partner for the show, it wouldn't be weird if you wore my jersey."

The smile she gives me takes my breath away, and it feels like when Ollie King from the Sasquatch runs into me.

"Thank you! Oh, Trevor, you're so sweet!"

I use the blade of my stick to raise the jerseys over the glass and she catches them as they fall down. I do it quickly so we don't get the crowd clamoring for freebies, and she scrambles back up to their seats. I'm keeping half an eye on them as I skate away, and Sophie is pulling my jersey on over her head. I like that she chose me over her brother.

The jerseys are huge on the girls. Sophie does something with a hair tie to bunch it up and make it cute. It would be even sexier if that was all she was wearing. Turning around and looking over her shoulder with a coy smile, so all I see is my last name and her smiling face. I don't know why that turns me on. I'm never giving a woman my last name. My branch of the family tree is sprouting no limbs.

Speaking of my last name, I realize it was just announced, and the crowd is cheering while I'm staring at Sophie and fantasizing about things I'd like to do with her. Reluctantly, I tear my gaze away and acknowledge the cheers. I'm here as one of the best players in the league, and I should be focused on one thing alone. But the image of Sophie in my jersey and imagining her one day flashing me a come-hither smile over her shoulder has me half hard. Which is uncomfortable while wearing a cup.

"Look like you've been hitting the casino buffets there, Carter. Good luck hauling your fat carcass around the rink," Kel Fessel, a coyote shifter forward for the Omaha Ogres, chirps at me.

The other contestants around us laugh. I give him a good-natured shin tap back.

"Don't worry about me, Fessel. It's a shame they don't have a hot-dog-eating contest. At least then you'd have a chance to win something. Something to suggest for next year when the game's in Atlantic City."

One of the Colorado Cryptids players, a lion shifter, joins in.

"No one wants the Birds to win the Dickinson Cup, but a weekend in Atlantic City sounds fun."

"Hey, don't forget Vegas!" a fellow wolf shifter who plays for the Area 51 Aliens, says.

After a weekend in Vegas, chances are none of us would remember anything. We laugh then skate off in different directions to get things started.

My teammates perform well in their events. Stone's sister, Bridget "Brick" Waller, wins the goalie competition by stopping the most goals in a row. My team captain, Burke Bedard, is the champion of the hardest slapshot event.

It's my turn to skate, and I take some deep breaths to calm down. The adrenaline coursing through my veins can help me go faster—but it can also make me careless. It would be mortifying to lose an edge and wipe out in front of this crowd. I stand at the blue line until I get the signal to start. As I take my first strides and start to gather speed, I hear Randi and Sophie screaming for me, and it kicks me into a higher gear. It's pure freedom, circling the rink along the boards. It's the same feeling I have while running through the woods as my wolf. My blades dig into the ice, and the cadence of the swooshes soon matches the beat of my heart. I lean into the curves, staying as close to the cones marking the course as possible to shave every last millisecond off my time. In the end, I'm crowned the winner with the fastest time by more than a second.

After the race, I skate past Fessel, the runner-up, and say, "The all-you-can-eat lobster buffet we get really helps. All that butter keeps the joints lubricated, you know."

I wink at Sophie as I skate by on my victory lap with my stick held high. Randi's eyes widen and she glances between me and Sophie, a grin slowly spreading across her face. Whatever she's thinking, she's got the right idea. But Sophie and I don't need a matchmaker. Though after seeing her with my name on her back, I wouldn't say no to a hookup. And we can handle hooking up on our own. But that's all it can be. A hookup, a fling.

I'm not made for relationships.

Normally we aren't hanging out in the bar the night before a big game, but that's what most of us are doing tonight. We're at a high table, and I have my arm resting along the back of Randi's stool. I'm sticking to soda water with lime tonight, but Sophie and Randi both have margaritas. If they're drinking, there's no way I am. I feel like it's my responsibility to remain alert and keep them safe. I know I'm probably overreacting, and if it was just a Devil Birds party, I know I could let loose. But I don't know these people, so I'm not risking it.

Randi's telling us a story about working in New Zealand when she stops mid-sentence and sucks in a breath. I glance across the room and do a double-take. Mac's striding through the bar, and he's laser-focused on Randi. I hurriedly remove my arm from the back of her stool because I'm pretty sure Mac is ready to rip it off. Hard to hold a hockey stick with only one arm.

Suddenly, Mac's at our table. Randi whispers his name, and they're kissing like he's just come back from war. When they finally break apart, Randi stands from her stool. Without a word to anyone, or even a glance, Mac plows like a speedboat through the crowd, pulling Randi in his wake.

Daphne yells out "Yes!" in the stunned silence, and then everyone laughs and starts chattering.

Sophie and I turn to each other, wide-eyed.

"Are you sharing a room with Randi?" I ask. Because if she is, she's homeless now.

She shakes her head. "No, thank goodness. Walking in on them once was more than enough."

We burst out laughing, and when I hear Sophie's laugh is a mix of a chuckle and a wheeze, it only makes me laugh harder. She leans into my side, and I look down at her. She's looking up at me, and our lips are inches apart. Her breath catches. I don't know if I move, she moves, or we meet in the middle, but we're kissing and it's even better than New Year's because now I know how soft her lips are and how sweet she tastes. I could kiss her all night long, but I remember we're in a bar full of people we know from home and players from the other teams. Shit, we have to work together for the next two months.

Reluctantly, I pull back from the kiss. Blue eyes look up at me with a mixture of shock and lust. No doubt she sees the same in my hazel eyes. How can something that feels so good be such a bad idea?

"We shouldn't do that," she whispers.

I quirk up a corner of my mouth in a half-hearted grin. She's right. I agree with her completely. And I hate that. "I know. But it's fun."

The smile she gives me is glorious, and it's like I've been punched in the solar plexus.

Then the smile turns into a yawn, and an adorable flush creeps up her neck as she covers her mouth. "I'm sorry. I'm good with whisky, but fruity drinks like margaritas make me tipsy and sleepy."

I smile. "Don't apologize. I should turn in too. I know it's not a game that affects the standings tomorrow, but I still want to win. Ready to go upstairs?"

Those words are meant innocently, but the second they pass my lips, my mind flashes to all the things we can do upstairs. Not gonna happen. First of all, she's tipsy. I don't mess with tipsy girls. Second, we need to work together, and I don't think getting physical will make that any easier. Finally, I think I could like her. She can be prickly, and I don't think it was all because of the tea. But I get her. We probably have a lot in common. Maybe. Who knows? Maybe I'm just projecting. Whatever's going on, it would suck to torpedo things by rushing into something physical too quickly.

All the same, her blue eyes flash with an awareness that makes me think her mind is in the same place mine is. But, just like me, she's going to ignore it. For now.

I get up and grab Sophie's hand so we don't get separated as we weave through the crowd. For no good reason, I keep a hold of it as we cross the lobby to the elevators, and I hold it as we reach our floor and walk down the hall. I finally, reluctantly, let go when we get to our doors. Our rooms are across the hall from each other, and Randi's room is next to Sophie's. The nice thing about Clardmore hotels is that they're built with shifters in mind and have extra soundproofing in the rooms to be mindful of superior shifting hearing. Still, even if you don't actually hear anything, knowing your best friend and brother are in the next room boinking is awkward as hell.

"If you want to bunk in here," I say, "you can. No hanky-panky, just sleeping."

She grimaces, looks toward Randi's door, then swipes her key card and pushes open the door. With a jerk of her head, she invites me to follow her in. We stand there, facing each other with our heads cocked toward the common wall. We hear a faint cry of what I assume is ecstasy, and that's enough for Sophie to grab her bag and head toward the door.

"Let's go. We're only sleeping," she says as she yanks it open. Just as my sister and coach are walking by.

Mallory stops and looks at us and then down at Sophie's bag, her eyes widening in surprise.

"Going somewhere?" she asks. Then she notices me behind Sophie. Shit.

Coach looks at me with raised eyebrows.

"Miranda and Declan are next door. I just...no." Sophie shakes her head emphatically.

Mal's nose scrunches in commiseration.

Now Coach is smirking at me. "You know *your sister* and I have the room next to yours, right?"

Fuck my life.

Mal backhands Coach in the stomach, and he melodramatically groans and bends over like she hit him with a shovel.

"No worries," my sister says. "It's Liam's turn to wear the ball gag."

Sophie lets out a bark of laughter, but I swear I throw up in my mouth a bit.

My sister wiggles a finger between me and Sophie.

"Is there something going on with you two?" she asks.

"No!" we exclaim in unison, making her and Coach laugh.

"I'm sleeping on the couch," Sophie says.

Not what I was expecting to hear.

"You are?" I ask.

She looks at me like I'm insane.

"Aye, where else would I sleep? I'm not sharing a bed with you!"

For the first time, she's sounding Scottish and reminding me of her brother. Yeah, think about her brother, a man bigger and stronger than I am. One I consider a close friend. I have no intention of anything happening, no matter how attractive I may find her. We can share a bed, and I can control myself. Unless...maybe she can't control herself? A slow smile spreads across my face.

"Sleep well," Coach says, tugging Mallory toward their door.

"See you in the morning!" Mallory says with a big grin on her face.

I open the door and step back so Sophie can enter first. It's the same as her room—a king-size bed, a pull-out sofa bed, fridge, microwave, bathroom. It's nice but nothing special. I pull the cushions off the sofa.

"What are you doing?" Sophie asks.

I'd think it's obvious. "Making up the sofa bed?" I can't control the hesitation at the end of my sentence.

She shakes her head.

"I just need a pillow and a blanket. I'll be fine. I've slept on plenty of sofas," she says.

I know she's tiny, so she'll fit much better on the sofa than I will, but I'm too much of a gentleman to automatically take the bed. "No," I say, "You take the bed, and I'll take the couch."

She rolls her eyes. "You're being ridiculous, Trevor. You have an important hockey game tomorrow. You need to get a good night's sleep so you're well-rested. I'm fine on the sofa. Stop arguing with me." She gestures toward the bathroom. "Okay to use the bathroom to get changed, or do you want it first?"

I can tell by the stubborn set to her chin there's no point in arguing. I sweep a hand toward the bathroom. "Go ahead. I'll change out here."

She stops short on her trek to the bathroom. The way her gaze flickers down my body and then to the bed, paired with her cheeks going red makes me think that the fact that I'm going to be sleeping in something other than jeans and a T-shirt is just occurring to her. If I was alone, I'd be sleeping naked. If I wasn't alone, I'd be sleeping naked. But she's here, so I'll sleep in my boxer briefs. After a moment, she gives me a nod and goes into the bathroom. The click of the lock behind her sounds like a shotgun blast. I try not to take it personally. She doesn't know me, and it's most likely a habit. It's ridiculous to be offended by a locked bathroom door. What did I want her to do? Leave it wide open while she takes a crap? Stop being a goober, Trev.

Goober. I chuckle. I picked that up from my nephews. My older brother, Ethan, being perfect as usual, has two wonderful sons, EJ and Matt. I love those boys. The only thing he ever failed at was marriage, and that wasn't his fault. He would have stuck it out, but his ex-wife did them both a favor by recognizing they weren't happy and weren't going to be happy. She also loved the boys enough to realize their sons would be better off with Ethan having custody. I don't know that I could be that unselfish. That's part of the reason I'm never going to put myself in that position.

Speaking of positions, I grab a couple of pillows off my bed and get the bedding for the pull-out sofa from the closet. I don't care that Sophie says she'll be fine sleeping there. That can't be as comfortable as having the space of a bed. The least I can do is make it cozy. I'm just spreading the blanket as she leaves the bathroom.

"Trevor, you didn't have to do that. Thank you!"

I look up and my heart does the cha-cha dance I need to learn. She's fricking adorable in her white shorts with hearts that match her hot-pink tank top. I'm trying so hard not to look at her breasts, but it's difficult. They are high and firm. Not more than a handful, but that's plenty, as far as I'm concerned. Her long blonde hair is in a loose braid. What gets me are the fuchsia plastic eyeglass frames perched on her nose.

"You wear glasses," I say in wonder.

The rosy flush that floods her cheeks to match the frames is the cutest thing I've ever seen.

"Yeah." She pushes her glasses up her nose with her forefinger and looks down at the floor.

Crap, I didn't mean to make her feel self-conscious.

"Hey," I say softly, putting my finger under her chin to tip her face up to mine. "No looking down. Eyes up here." Her gorgeous blue eyes lift to mine. I let the goofy smile I should hide spread across my lips. "You have no idea how stinking cute you are in glasses. Of course you're beautiful. You must know that. But in glasses, you have that smexy thing happening that's irresistible."

Her nose crinkles and, oh my goodness, she has freckles on her nose. Her makeup hides them, and that's probably a good thing because I've got the urge to kiss every single one of them. I never knew glasses and freckles were my kryptonite, but apparently, they are.

"Smexy?" she asks.

"Smart and sexy."

"Oh."

Her flush deepens, and I'm grateful I'm still in my jeans. The reaction I'm having down below would be way too obvious if I were only in my boxer briefs. How am I supposed to handle being so close to her all night and not being able to touch her? Inspiration strikes.

"Would it bother you if I took a shower?" I ask.

Now it's her eyes widening. I wonder if she's thinking about me wet and naked in the shower. The cold shower. I wonder if she's aware she's the reason I need to take it.

"No, do whatever you need to! This is your room. Thank you for making up the sofa for me. That's so sweet."

She shocks the hell out of me by climbing up on the sofa bed and holding onto my shoulder so she can lean over and give me a kiss on the cheek. It's taking all of my willpower to not turn my head so our lips meet. Again.

I stand like a statue until I'm sure she's steady and then step away.

Clearing my throat, I nod. "You're welcome." There I go again, being a goober.

I grab a clean pair of briefs and some gray sweatpants and head into the bathroom. I take my shower, and though I try to be a good man, I'm not a saint. I can't help but think of Sophie as I grasp my hard cock and start rubbing it. No time for indulging in any elaborate fantasies or savoring the experience. I do what's necessary to get the release I need, swallowing a groan of satisfaction as my cum washes down the drain. After doing a quick lather and rinse, I turn off the water and step out. Briskly drying myself, I listen for the TV or any other sound from the bedroom. Nothing. I pull on my black boxer briefs and gray sweatpants and crack open the door. Sophie's under the covers on the sofa bed.

I pad over to the bed and make sure my alarm is set. Dropping my sweatpants, I slide under the blankets with a sigh. The Clardmore is pure class, and the billion thread count sheets they use are the softest thing I've ever felt against my skin. I need to find out the brand and get them for my bed at home. I roll to my side, close my eyes, and then I hear it. Tiny little snores that remind me of Cooper, the Bernese mountain dog puppy Coach got Mallory for Christmas. He's an adorable bundle of black, brown, and white fluff that you can't help but love. When he's asleep in his crate, he lets out puppy snores, and that's exactly what Sophie sounds like. If she let out the puppy farts Cooper's becoming famous for, it would be easier to resist her, but no such luck. With a smile on my face, I close my eyes and drift off to sleep.

4

SOPHIE

TREVOR'S TEAM IS WINNING. OF COURSE THEY ARE. I NEVER WOULD'VE guessed that Miranda is some sort of coaching genius, but she came out of nowhere with incredible plays. She's the coach's assistant in terms of scheduling and that sort of thing. Actually coaching the team isn't part of her job. But here she is, calling plays. They're scoring goals, and she's getting hugs and high fives from all the players. Honestly, I'm happy for her. She's smiling more than she has since I've been here. She's glowing, and it's not because of sex with my brother.

I feel like that when a piece I've choreographed is danced perfectly. Even more than when I dance it myself. I love dancing. It's all I've ever wanted to do. It's all I can do. I'm not athletic like Declan or smart like my other brothers. My twin, Ian, is a more successful dancer than I am because he has more charisma. I may perform the steps perfectly, but Ian is so entertaining, no one cares if it's not perfect. My younger brother is a charmer—everyone loves him. But dance is all I have going for me.

The final horn sounds, and Trevor's team wins. They hug and shake hands. One of the Devil Birds players, Nathan Crosby, wins

Most Valuable Player and is awarded a new SUV. When pop sensation Amilia Reynolds hands him the key, he's so flustered he drops it. Apparently, he has a huge crush on her. It's kind of adorable to see this big professional athlete who's one of the best in the world be a star-struck fool like the rest of us. The crowd laughs good-naturedly as the poor guy flushes scarlet and squats down to pick it up. Trevor gives him a clap on his shoulder when he rises back to his full height. Whatever Trevor whispered to him has them both grinning. It's cute.

"What do you think he said to Crosby?" Daphne asks from where she stands between me and Mallory along the glass.

"As his sister, probably something I don't want to know," Mallory answers. "I feel sorry for you having to work with him, Sophie. I hope he takes it seriously. I love my brother. He's a great guy, but he thinks everything is a joke."

Daphne furrows her brow. "I don't think that's fair, Mallory. Yeah, he's lighthearted and a bit of a goof, but he takes hockey seriously. He takes his friendships with Kendall and Randi seriously. He'd do anything for either of them. He took passing the bar exam seriously. He's grown up a lot recently. I think you're too close to see it."

"He's twenty-five years old. It's about time he grows up. He's more of a puppy than Cooper."

"Who's Cooper?" I ask.

"Oh, he's my Bernese mountain dog puppy! Liam gave him to me for Christmas. He's adorable. Here, let me show you."

She whips out her phone and starts showing me picture after picture of a drooling dog. He's cute, but I don't need to see a whole album. Then there's a picture of two puppies, two boys, and Trevor. He's lying on the floor, laughing, boys and puppies all piled on top of him.

"Those are my nephews, EJ—" she points to an older boy, "—and Matt." She points to the younger one. "The puppy with the green bow is theirs. They named her Heidi. She's Cooper's sister."

"Trevor's having the time of his life," Daphne says, smiling at the picture.

Mallory looks up from the screen to see if I'm done looking. When I nod, she puts her phone away. "He is. He loves those boys. He's going to be a wonderful dad someday when he settles down. He's so good with kids."

I feel a twinge when she says that. It's confirming what I already know, but it still sucks to hear it's true. Doesn't matter. He's only my dance partner. There's no future, so no point even thinking about it.

With the presentations over, we follow the crowd out of the stands and join the team families. When we're all there, we go to the buses to meet the players and team staff that are waiting for us. I follow Daphne and Mallory and continue down the aisle after they sit next to their guys. My plan is to take the first open seat because it's awkward as hell to not really know anyone and try to fit in.

"Sophie, I saved a seat for you!" Trevor booms from the back.

A wave of *oohs* flows through the bus like we're back in primary school.

As heat rises up my neck, I curse my fair Irish skin and the obvious blush. There's no gracious way to say no, so I trudge to the back and sit next to him. "Thanks for saving me a seat. Congratulations on winning the game."

The smile he gives me is so boyishly sweet, my heart stutters a bit. He's a good-looking man. It's natural to be attracted to him. It doesn't mean anything. "Did you enjoy it? It was so cool! I love things like this and competing against the best. You know how it is, you're a competitive person."

That brings me up short. Am I a competitive person? I want to be noticed. I don't care about winning except for the fact that the winner's who people remember. No one remembers the silver medalist. But I don't want to win just to say I'm the best. I care about winning the show because that's how I'm going to get the pro spot. I don't want to keep being a background dancer. Background dancers don't get to choreograph.

I don't know how to explain that to Trevor, so I just nod. "Yeah. I know how it is."

The buses pull up to the terminal so we can board the team plane back to New Jersey. We didn't practice at all during this trip so it wasn't necessary I come along but I can't say I regret it. Trevor and I looked at our phones until we reached the airport, and now that we're on our way back to New Jersey, I'm sitting by myself and taking a nap. I wake up as the plane touches down, and I find Trevor sleeping beside me. I nudge him awake, and we keep each other upright as we leave the plane. Once we're in the cool night air, he looks down at me, yawning.

"You want to practice tonight?" he asks as we zoom through the winter evening along the Atlantic City Expressway on yet another bus.

I look at him in surprise. "Aren't you tired after the game?" Even though it meant nothing in the standings, I know the players took it seriously. Trevor had some hard hits and trips, even from his own teammate. I know it's important to allow your body to rest after heavy exertion.

"Soph, I'm going to be tired for the next two months. I'm going to have games and practices the whole time we're doing the show. If you don't want to practice, that's fine. We'll start tomorrow. It's your call."

I'm impressed with his willingness to work. "Sure. We can start with the basics in my room, if that's okay? No point getting lights on in the theater or studio. We'll go over the music and start with the first counts. The dance is ninety seconds. There will be about twenty or twenty-one eight counts of choreography. Do you think you'll be okay learning that?"

"Yeah, no problem. Not going to lie, it takes a lot of repetition for me to get choreo, but I eventually get it. I'm better at freestyle. But

I'll learn it. I promise to practice until I drop. If they make me do this competition, then I'm winning it. Second place is a waste of time and effort."

As the streets of Atlantic City pass by in a blur of traffic and street lights outside the window, I see both competitive spirit and sincerity in his hazel eyes. It does funny things to me. My tummy flips, and I feel like my heart does a happy little cha-cha. *Not good, Sophie.* Not good.

When we get off the bus, I expect him to swing by the parking garage so he can drop off his luggage before heading to my room. Instead, he takes my bag, along with his, and follows me upstairs. He catches my questioning glance and shrugs.

"Why waste time going back and forth? The sooner we get upstairs, the sooner we practice. You were saying how every minute counts. We dance as long as we can, and then I either go home or call down to the desk. If there's a room, they'll give it to me."

"That's convenient," I say as we walk down the hallway.

He nods. "One of the perks of being on the team."

After unlocking the door to my suite, I grab my suitcase from Trevor and wheel it into the bedroom.

"You're welcome to use the bathroom if you want to change into something more comfortable to dance in," I call over my shoulder. He's in slacks, dress shoes, and a button-down shirt. We aren't doing anything too crazy, but with the way his clothes are tailored to fit his muscular body to perfection, I'm not sure how freely he can move without ripping something. Would be a shame to ruin clothes that fit his body like a second skin. I bite my lip then shake my head. No, no. I'm not admiring Trevor. Just his tailor. Not that big, beautiful body. Just the way his clearly talented tailor fits it. Yeah, that's all I'm doing.

I change into a T-shirt and capri leggings. I shouldn't be ashamed of noticing Trevor's form. It's natural to appreciate an attractive man. He's good-looking, funny, well liked. I've seen enough showmances to know that working with someone hours a day for weeks and months creates an intoxicating intimacy. We haven't been together enough yet for anything to develop, but with the way I can sense him in a room, how I react to his woodsy, manly scent, my comfort with his hands on me, the way we kiss...whoa, can't think about these things. I know the show's producers love it when there are hints of romance brewing. It's helped a few couples win the competition. But I don't want to win for any reason other than talent. I'm sure Trevor will get votes because he's charming and good-looking. Maybe there will be hockey fans watching. But I want our team to win because we're the best. Because *I'm* the best.

But to be the best, we need to practice. So, I pull my hair back into a ponytail and wander out to the seating area of the suite. Trevor changed into shorts and a T-shirt and is sitting on the sofa, tying his sneakers. I grab my laptop and a couple of bottles of water for us and plop on the cushion next to him. I'm a professional dancer. I should be graceful. But I try not to lie, so I have to admit I plopped.

"Okay," I say, opening my laptop and settling back against the tan cushions of the sofa. "You know we have the cha-cha. We heard the song. There's a live band, and they play a portion of the song. We're going to learn the dance by count, not by the music. Are you okay with that?"

He grimaces. "Yeah. It's going to take a lot of repetition, though. For dancing, it's all about the music for me. I feel it and then move. What I did with counts were the cheers and stunts. They aren't fluid like a dance. I'm sorry."

I appreciate his candor. "How do you learn hockey plays? You have plays, right?"

He nods.

"Well, how do you learn them?"

His shrug is...uncertain. I don't know how to describe it. He's reacting because I'm expecting him to. Not a good start. "We practice them. Repetition."

"But no music?"

His brows draw together. "Of course not. It's hockey, not figure skating."

My turn to do acrobatics with my brows. Where his went down, mine go up.

"No," I say with a shake of my head, "it's not. But it's choreography in its own way."

He tilts his head from left to right, his lips quirking to the side. "Yeah." He nods slowly. "I guess it is."

I mentally add a tick mark to my side of the scoreboard. "So we'll treat our counts like plays, and each dance is a playbook." I'm proud of myself for talking all sporty. My brothers would be amazed. "You watch video to learn about your opponents and what you're doing, right?"

He nods.

Tapping my laptop, I settle back on the couch and rest it on my lap. "We're going to watch some videos so you can get an idea of the dance and the moves required. Hopefully that will help you when we learn the counts. Okay?"

"Aren't we going to dance? I thought that was the point." He cracks open his water and takes a sip. I try not to stare as his throat ripples with a swallow. Unlike many of his teammates, he doesn't have a beard, but his jaw has a dusting of stubble along it this late in the day. It's sexy. And not something I should be noticing.

"We will, but if you know how it's supposed to look, it may help you understand what I'm trying to teach you."

He lifts a shoulder, which I take as agreement, so I start the video playlist I created a few days ago. "Hey, that's you!" He grins. "Is that your brother? Ian?"

"It is. We were dance partners most of our lives. We competed until he switched to another partner and then made the show."

Trevor's brow furrows. "He dumped you as his partner? That would make Thanksgiving awkward."

"We're Irish, we don't do Thanksgiving," I say with a deadpan expression.

He gives a huff of exasperation and rolls his eyes. "St. Patrick's Day then."

Bless his clueless little brain.

Shrugging both physically and mentally, trying to dislodge the lingering hurt that's stirred by thinking about the end of my partnership with Ian, I say, "It was necessary. He had a growth spurt. I didn't. We weren't a good match any longer. For competitive dancing, a height difference of more than a foot is less than ideal."

"But you're his sister, his twin. How can he just switch because you're short?" He waves his hand between us. "There's more than a foot difference between us, even if you're in heels. They paired us up."

I sigh. "That's part of the challenge and a source of drama. They want to make sure we have difficulty and something to be frustrated about. Makes for good television."

A laugh rumbles from his chest, making his shoulders shake. "Like they need to give us reasons to fight with each other. I think we're going to butt heads well enough on our own without a few inches coming between us."

I bet he's more than a few inches. My cheeks heat. I know he meant inches of height, but he said "coming," and I grew up with brothers who made crude jokes and innuendos every chance they had. They still do, if I'm being completely honest. I cannot be blamed for my naughty thoughts.

"You think we're going to fight?" I ask. Logically, that shouldn't hurt, but no one's going to accuse me of being the most logical person in the room.

Trevor's eyes widen like he's realized he misspoke. I hope he can dance as well as he can backpedal.

"No, of course not! I think we're going to work together wonderfully. No friction. All smooth sailing."

I bump him with my shoulder. "It's okay. I know I can be a pain in the arse to deal with. Ian and I would drive each other nuts. That's part of the reason we stopped working together. We would've ended up hating each other. I love my twin. As much as I love dancing, I love him more. So we split."

He reaches over to hit pause on the video. We missed it anyway. "Did you find another partner? Did you keep competing?"

Admitting this is humiliating. "I tried. Ian had dancers lined up, hoping to be picked. Not the same for me. I tried with a couple of partners, but we didn't click. They said I was difficult to work with and too bossy. Ian was winning major international competitions. Not shifter competitions, professional dance competitions against the very best in the world. He was picked for the show, and he made me a condition of his contract—they had to give me a tryout."

Trevor's brow furrows. I'm sure he's regretting being stuck with me. The only reason I'm on the show is because of nepotism.

"Between our mother judging and Ian dancing, they kind of had to give me a shot." I shove my laptop onto Trevor's lap and rise so I can pace. I'm too aggravated to sit still. "I'm a good dancer. Yeah, I can be bossy, but I can dance! I deserved to audition based on my own merits and not as a favor or a condition. But that's how it worked out, and now everyone thinks of me as some sort of nepo baby, the dancer who can only get jobs because of her family connections. Not my talent."

He puts the laptop on the coffee table in front of him, rises, and walks over to me. Trevor doesn't say anything, but when he pulls me into a hug, he doesn't have to. His compassion and understanding are clear in his embrace. Our height difference may make dancing together a challenge, but the way his big body cradles mine makes me feel cherished and protected. I'm always around men much larger than I am. My father and brothers are all large men. All my potential dance partners and former romantic partners have been too. I'm used to big guys. Sometimes it's overwhelming. As a wolf shifter, I can protect myself if necessary, so the size disparity usually isn't an issue in terms of safety, but it's something I'm aware of.

But Trevor's size doesn't overwhelm me. It comforts me. Just like waking up in his room this morning, I felt safe knowing he was there even though he was across the room from me. I want to burrow into his heat and his solid body, but I can't. We need to focus on dancing. Reluctantly, I pull out of his embrace.

"As someone who hears that he only has his spot on the team because of his sister's relationship with one of the owners, who also happens to be my coach, I know how you feel."

My nose scrunches like I'm smelling bullshit. "That's ridiculous. You're a talented player. You played in the All-Star Game. You didn't get picked for that honor because of who your sister's shagging."

His shrug is half-hearted. "That's what I tell myself, and I know I'm good. But it's still disheartening. I feel like I need to work four times as hard to prove that I'm at least half as good as everyone else."

"Yes!" He gets it. When I've tried to explain it before, I'd get placated. *Don't be silly*, they'd say, with a side of *boo-hoo, poor little rich girl not getting what she wants.*

The look we share is one of understanding. I haven't had that with someone before. And I can't have that now. We're dance partners. A team for two months, and then he's focused on hockey and I need to focus on my career as a pro. Get a spot on the tour they usually do after the shows. I'll be the Mackenzie in the spotlight for once.

But first, we need to learn the cha-cha.

"Come on," I say, retaking my seat on the couch and picking up my laptop. "Let's watch these dances so we can start learning counts tomorrow. We go to New York for the morning show the day after tomorrow for the announcement and introduction. They'll take measurements so they can start on costumes. Yours will be basic pants and shirts. Unless you drop a ton of weight or gain massive amounts of muscle, they won't bother you much except for final fittings. And spray tans."

That stops his descent to the cushion next to me. His thigh muscles are incredibly impressive in the semi-squat position he's frozen in. "Spray tans? Are you serious?"

"Absolutely, we all get them. No one wants to have tan lines or pasty skin. It reflects the lights weird, plus they can do wonders with shading to enhance muscle tone."

He finally sits next to me and quirks a brow.

"Not that you'd need any enhancements, I'm sure," I say, both placatingly and honestly.

Predator shifters like wolves normally have superior muscle tone naturally. If that shifter works out regularly, especially at an intense level like that of a professional athlete, their body looks like they've been sculpted by Michaelangelo. No need to fake a six-pack with strategically placed darker stripes of tanning spray.

He runs a fingertip along my arm, and goosebumps erupt. His brows lift. I'm wrong. I keep calling his eyes hazel, but they're so much more than that. Besides green and brown, there are shades of gray in there too. They're beautiful.

"Is this your tan?" he asks.

I shrug. "I've been getting spray tans for so long I think I'm permanently stained." I hold my arm next to his. He's about the same shade as I am.

"Turn your arm over," I direct.

He does as I say. I can see the blue veins under his skin. And a scar.

"What happened?" I trace the ten-centimeter scar. It's old, a smooth white line now, but it doesn't look like it was a minor injury.

Trevor sighs, and I raise my gaze from where it's studying his arm to his face. Now there are gray clouds where there was green previously.

"I got slashed by a skate blade when I was a kid. I was lucky. It could've been so much worse, but I had to have a bunch of stitches. Having shifter genes helped immensely. If I was only human, the scar would've been a lot more gnarly."

"How old were you?"

"Ten."

Tears flood my eyes. He was a little boy. That must have been so scary.

"Hey," he says softly, cupping my cheek and using his thumb to wipe away the tear that escapes. "I'm okay. It worked out great. Mom invented a cut-resistant fabric that's now standard. All the kids in our junior hockey program are provided it for free."

My heart melts. "Your mother loves you so much she invented something to keep you safe." I give a hiccuping sob. "And it protects other children so they don't get hurt like you did. That's beautiful."

"It made her company a shit ton of money, she got a promotion, and the value of her stash of company stock skyrocketed. I wouldn't call her selfless."

Being a pragmatic soul, I shrug. "No reason everyone can't benefit."

His deep chuckle does things to me, like when I do the never-ending spins in salsa. It's not unpleasant, just...strange.

"Let's get to know each other," he says. "Where do you fall in the birth order of your family? You're the only girl, right?"

"I'm the second-youngest, only girl. Dec is the oldest, and he's always been the leader. Patrick and Owen are best friends with each other and have the twin thing going. Ian and I are twins, but I'm the only girl, so I'm on the outside. We have dance in common and similar taste in guys—Ian's gay—but it's not the same twin connection. Seamus is the youngest, and he's less than a year younger than me and Ian, so it was almost like we were triplets, with Ian and Seamus being best friends."

Trevor cocks his head and studies me. What's he thinking? Of course I'm on the outside because it's obvious there's something wrong with me and that's why I'm kept in the shadows? But I want to shine. I want to be noticed.

"I get it. I'm the youngest of four. I'm almost five years younger than Mallory. Valerie and Mallory are only ten months apart."

"Did people think they were twins because they were close in age and had rhyming names?"

"Maybe? I don't know. Ethan is eighteen months older than Valerie. They were the closest. Mallory and I are close. We're all wolf shifters except Mallory. She can't shift. That made her an outsider. I was an oops baby. I'm eight years younger than Ethan, so we didn't hang out. Our parents were heavily involved in their careers by the time I came along. Mom was a chemical engineer, and Dad was a patent attorney. That's how I ended up involved with dance and cheerleading. I was with my cousins all the time, and my aunts and uncles would just include me in whatever activities their kids were doing. I didn't want to do baseball because that was Ethan's thing, and I didn't want to be in his shadow."

I hold my hand up for a high five.

"I guess you know about being in the shadows?" he asks.

"I'm in the shadows so much I never need sunscreen," I joke.

Trevor stands and takes my hand, pulling me into a dance hold. "You, Sophie Mackenzie, should always be in the spotlight." He twirls me around.

It's very sweet of him and kinda romantic, but he's doing it all wrong. I can't help it, I have to correct him.

"Left hand up," I tell him. Facing him, I place my right hand in his left and my left hand on the upper part of his right arm. "Your right hand at my left shoulder blade."

Looking in the mirror, I see he's close. "Just a smidge higher. And stand up straight. I know you're tall, but I'll be in heels. You'll have a heel of either one or one and a half inches, depending on if you're wearing a standard or Cuban heel."

"I'm not wearing a Cuban heel," Trevor insists, looking down at me.

"Do you even know what a Cuban heel is?"

"No, but I know I don't want to wear them."

I pull out of his hold and jam my fists on my hips. "You have a dance background. You know you must wear the proper gear. You wouldn't play hockey without your pads. You're going to wear Cuban heels on the show."

He lifts his chin in the direction of my laptop, so I open it and restart the video.

"I need to move to learn," he says. "I can't just sit here and watch other people do it."

We try the moves, and he usually gets them wrong. And we laugh. He's trying, but he wasn't kidding when he said it takes repetition for him to learn. Amazingly, I'm not as frustrated as I expected to be. I'm not a patient teacher. I can see clearly what I want the dance to be and can demonstrate it or show examples on video, but I can't explain it clearly enough to teach it to someone who finds the moves unfamiliar. I know Trevor can learn the dances, given enough time and practice. My concern is if I'm going to be able to teach them to him.

He wants to try again, but I suggest we go back to watching the videos. Hopefully knowing what it's supposed to look like will help him learn the dance. He gives me puppy dog eyes that I can't resist, so I agree to try one last time, and then it's back to video. I start the counts and...he does it. He hits every single step of the twenty-four counts I've taught him. I'm breathless when we hit the final count. Our bodies are pressed together. And he's hard. How the hell was he able to dance with that happening? Our eyes meet, and we break apart like we were caught snogging by my parish priest.

My yawn is only partly fake as I check the time on my laptop. "Oh, shit, it's after midnight." I yawn again to punctuate my sentence. "I'm sorry, Trevor. You must be exhausted. You had a longer day than I did."

"I'm okay. I'll get a room, not a big deal."

He worked up a sweat while we were dancing, and his scent is intoxicating. He smells like pine trees and vanilla. That's unexpected. But there's also the underlying notes of his natural scent. It's not something I can narrow down to specific scent notes, it's just him. Longing pools in my abdomen, and my nipples tighten with desire.

It's biology, Soph, I tell myself. We're both wolf shifters. Catching his scent all the time is distracting. He's a good-looking man even without being a wolf shifter. But with us both being wolf shifters of an age where our mating drives are at their highest, we're going to be drawn to each other. And that's the problem. I'm nobody's mate.

Maybe he'd be okay with a physical relationship. We scratch our itches, and when he finds a mate, or I tire of him, we move on. It's possible that could help our connection on the dance floor. Rather than working to stay separate, we could lean into the attraction and bond. It's only a couple of months, and then we'll be apart anyway. He'll travel with the team to finish their season. I'll hopefully be invited on the tour with the pros from the other shows, and then I'll be busy working with my next partner and filming.

"Or," I say, trying to keep the hesitation from my voice, "you could just stay here. It's silly to bother the staff." Maybe he wants to be away from me. I know I can be a lot. Crap. I'm making things awkward. "Unless you'd rather have your own space."

He quirks his lips at my babbling. "Is there a second room?"

My face flushes scarlet. There obviously isn't. He can see everything from where we're standing. "No. I was thinking you could stay in my room. In my bed. With me." His raised eyebrows have me rushing to add, "I'm not saying we're having sex, but we could fool around and cuddle."

He nods slowly and gives me a panty-melting grin. "Okay. Just so you know, I don't expect anything. Anytime you want to send me to the couch or another room, that's fine."

I know I can trust him. I shouldn't have confidence in instincts that have led me astray before, but I do.

"I know. This doesn't mean anything. It's just scratching an itch. My wolf likes to cuddle. Does yours?"

He nods.

I take a deep breath, which fills my lungs with his scent again. That doesn't help my resolve to only cuddle and not have sex. "No sex tonight. But we're both single and like kissing each other."

That sexy smile turns up a notch as he nods again.

"And we're going to be too busy to deal with anyone else. I'm sure we both have needs, and it's a convenient way to scratch them.

So maybe we'll have sex sometime. But it's just for our time on the show. It's just temporary. A fling."

His chuckle settles over me like a cozy blanket. I want to snuggle in and get comfy.

"You can change your mind, Sophie. It's okay to say something impulsively and then wish you could take it back." The sincerity in Trevor's voice is soothing.

"No! I don't want to take it back." Blowing out a breath and shaking my hands, I try to decide how honest to be. "I'm nervous. Obviously, we're attracted to each other."

"Obviously."

I roll my eyes. "I think you're hot, I'm horny, I want to fuck you, but I'm only interested in a fling. No relationship, no falling in love, no future. Just have fun for now. If you're good with that, I think we can enjoy each other."

Trevor nods his head vigorously, like a bobblehead in an earthquake. "I'm good with that. Yeah. So good."

I lead us into the bedroom. "You can have the bathroom first if you want."

As Trevor disappears into the bathroom with his bag, I close the bedroom door and push away from it. I try to ignore the sounds of him getting ready for bed and taking a shower. It's not my fault my shifter senses are so acute I can hear everything and that I have a vivid imagination. It's my job to be able to look at a person and envision how they move.

I pull on my pj's and go to the small powder room in the suite to brush my teeth and take out my contacts. No sex until after our first week on the show. If we don't get past the first dance, having a sexual relationship will be messy. Yeah, that's practical. There's plenty we can do still. And maybe dangling that carrot will get us through the cha-cha.

The shower is still running as I slide into bed. I don't know what side Trevor sleeps on, so I pick what I prefer, and we'll work it out.

My goodness, is he going to leave any hot water for the rest of the guests? Good thing I take showers in the morning. May as well get comfy while I wait. He better be worth it.

5

TREVOR

I DIDN'T PLAN TO TAKE SO LONG IN THE SHOWER, BUT I HAD TO RELIEVE THE ache in my balls and jerk off. Twice. No way could I sleep beside Sophie, touching her, smelling her, and not want her. I hear the snores as I open the bathroom door. She's asleep. Her pink glasses on the nightstand bring a smile to my lips. How many people have seen her wear them? I have the feeling not many, and that makes me happy. She's on her side, facing the center of the bed. Her hands are sweetly tucked under her cheek. My bedside lamp is on and washing over her in gentle light, and my heart flutters. It must be heartburn. It can't be anything more than that. This is a no-strings fling. Of course there are feelings, but there can't be *feelings*. I slide between the sheets and turn off the light. I'm trying to decide whether to pull Sophie into my arms or give her space when she scooches toward me. I lift my arm, and she settles against me, resting her head on my shoulder and draping an arm over my bare abdomen. Her breathing has remained steady, and her eyes are closed. I think she's still asleep. She has to be exhausted. I know I am.

This is my first time sleeping with a woman. I've had sex, of course, but I've never shared a bed and slept through the night, waking up next to my partner. This will be a first, especially since we didn't even have sex or make out. I press a kiss to the crown of her head and close my eyes to let sleep overtake me.

The winter sun slants weakly through the window. I watch the sun rise over the Atlantic Ocean, a rare treat. I love living out in the woods, but there's something about being near the ocean that brings me peace. Especially on January mornings like this, when the beach is empty, the quality of the light is muted, and there's a dusting of snow on the sand. It's magical.

I turn off my alarm before it sounds. No reason to break the peace with its annoying tone. Sophie is still cuddled up against me. My arm is asleep under her head, and I'm sore from not changing positions all night, but I wouldn't disturb her for anything. I hope she slept well. My dick isn't the only thing stirring, having her so warm and close to me. My wolf is stirring because he caught her scent. It's hormones, not feelings. We're both young, attractive, healthy wolf shifters of mating age. Nature is forcing me to take notice of her. But it doesn't matter if I—as a man or as my wolf—find her attractive. We can't be with her for anything more than a fling.

She and I cleared the air some, and I understand where she's coming from. Her goals as a dancer are as precious to her as my hockey goals are to me. We both have a lot to prove, and we must work together to do that. We need to work in harmony to find our groove and win the Platinum Paw. I chuckle quietly to myself. Listen to me with all the dance clichés. Kennie and Randi would laugh their asses off if they knew my thoughts.

My chuckle must have roused her because a sleep-flushed Sophie sighs and cuddles closer.

"Good morning," she says, her Irish lilt strong and washing over me like a gentle mist.

"Good morning." Everything in me wants to lower my head and

press a kiss to her strawberry lips, but I resist. It's not only in dancing that I'm taking cues from Sophie. After what we discussed last night, I understand her need for control. I think if we're going to be successful, I'm going to need to let her be the alpha in this partnership. Yeah, I give off an air of being easygoing and uncaring, but that's not true. I like to be in control too. But if letting her lead is what's necessary in this dance, so be it. It's only two months, not forever.

A beautiful smile spreads across her face, like the sun coming out from behind a cloud. It's glorious, and warmth spreads through me.

"Did you sleep well?" she asks.

"Um...yeah." I hope that's the right answer, and that I kept the inflection of my response neutral enough that it didn't turn into a question.

The smile doesn't disappear, and she nods her head in agreement, so it must have been an appropriate answer.

"Me too. Don't tell my mother, but I think the beds here are even more comfortable than those in the Clardmore hotels."

"Your secret's safe with me." Any and all of them.

Can't help it, she's irresistible. Slowly, I lower my mouth to hers, giving her plenty of opportunity to stop me. She doesn't. Sophie raises her face to meet mine, and our lips cling sweetly. I don't deepen it, just caress her lips with mine. I don't rush it because it's like watching the winter sun rise over the snowy beach—a rare treat I never want to end. My heart races but is also entirely content to let my body set a slow pace. Everywhere her soft hands flutter with gentle touches, my skin ignites with pleased fascination. It needs more, and so do I, but before I can take it, she pulls away. It's my first good morning kiss. I've had dozens, probably hundreds, of good night kisses, but this is my first good morning. I'd be sad about what I missed out on, but I think because it's with Sophie that it's this pleasurable.

Sophie's soft sigh as my lips lift from hers tempts me to go in for round two, but if I do that, we're not getting out of this bed for hours, and there's too much I need to do before dance practice this afternoon and my game tonight. She must agree because she wiggles out of my embrace and sits up. She squints toward the bedside clock before reaching for her glasses on the table and settling them on her nose.

"How long have you had glasses?" I ask.

"Since I was twelve or thirteen. When I started shifting, it became obvious I had issues with distance vision."

I furrow my brow. "How does that work as your wolf? You can wear glasses or contacts as a human, you can't do that as your wolf."

She shrugs. "That's why I say my wolf is decorative, not functional. She's not blind or running into trees, but she wouldn't get a driving license."

That makes me chuckle. I've only seen her in wolf form once, but it made an impression. She's gorgeous. I can picture her behind the wheel of a convertible with her silvery fur blowing in the breeze. Just like in her human form, she's petite but powerful. No matter her shape or form, she's beautiful and has a presence that commands my attention as both a man and a wolf.

"You're okay with me taking a shower before we head to your place? I don't want to slow you down," Sophie says as she gets out of bed.

"Take the time you need, Soph, it's okay. Do you want me to make coffee or something?"

She shakes her head. "I have juice in the fridge. Make some for yourself though."

When I hear the shower turn on, I get out of bed and pull on joggers and a T-shirt before going to the powder room to brush my teeth. I grab a bottle of water and scroll on my phone until Sophie is ready. Then I open the door and sweep my arm in invitation for her to exit before me.

Pulling the door closed behind me, I try the handle to make sure the lock is engaged. It's a habit. I always do things like that and checking the knobs on the stove. Making sure my sisters' curling irons are unplugged. I know everyone thinks I'm a bit of a goof, but I'm a cautious person at heart. She hits the button on the elevator, and we head down to the pedestrian bridge to the parking garage where my BMW is parked.

Shifter males are usually taller and larger than the average human male, so owning bigger, heavier vehicles makes sense. But ever since I was a boy and first dreamed of being an attorney, having a flashy sports car was part of the image I had for myself.

Lawyers on TV always had the tailored suits and the sexy cars. My father is an attorney, but he deals with patents. If station wagons were still a thing, he'd drive one. Instead, he's in a very reliable fifteen-year-old Honda that's so plain and nondescript, it's probably invisible to traffic cameras. Not that Dad would ever run a stop sign or speed or park illegally.

He's been wearing the same suits for twenty years. "Function over fashion" is what I heard all of my life. It's silly to buy new suits when the ones you have still fit. The classics never go out of style. Vanity is a sign of immaturity. Why pay twice as much just to look good? My BMW is my way of being my own man and fulfilling my human dreams more than catering to my shifter comfort.

No reason trying to explain that to my teammates. It would be something new for them to razz me about. They'll claim it's making up for an inferiorly sized penis or some nonsense like that. They share a locker room with me, and we've all seen each other naked. I have absolutely nothing to make up for.

"Are you excited to go to New York this week?" I ask as I drive us to my home.

There's no stopping the grin stretching across her face.

"I am," she says, doing a little bounce in her seat. "I've watched Ian do the contestant introductions and interviews as a pro dancer the past few years, and it seems so exciting. When I've been on the telly before, it's just been for dancing, I haven't spoken on camera. I probably won't be asked anything at the announcement, but I've had media training. That was part of what I had to do to get the spot this season. Our meeting on New Year's and our rehearsals will be edited, so less stressful."

She gasps and puts her hand on my thigh. "You're not camera-shy, are you?"

I cover her hand on my leg and give it a light squeeze. "No worries, I'm fine on camera. I'm comfortable with public speaking. I did mock trials and moot court in law school, plus interviews for the Devil Birds. We had media training too."

She lets out a sigh of relief. I'm glad I can take that stress off her shoulders.

We arrive at my home without incident. I feed us, get my dirty clothes into the wash, and then we head to the studio in the barn to stretch and warm up. The last thing I need is to tear a muscle dancing so I can't play hockey.

"Okay, ready?" Sophie asks. Her sweater is falling off her shoulder, and seeing the strap of the gray tank underneath and the creamy skin of her shoulder is distracting.

I could kiss that shoulder, nibble it where it joins her neck just to see what she tastes like. "Yeah, let's do this."

"Let's start with the counts we worked on last night."

Darn. Sophie interprets "this" to mean continuing to learn our first dance.

We try to get through the twenty-four counts that I successfully learned last night, but I can't even make it past the first eight this morning to her satisfaction. She shows me the steps, and I do them. And I do them again. And again. It's eight counts. I can count to eight quite successfully. But according to Sophie's standard, the concept of numbers and counting must be completely foreign to me. Apparently I've never moved my body in any kind of coordinated manner. She's getting frustrated, and frankly, so am I.

"How about we move on to the next eight counts?" I suggest.

"Why?" she says from inside her sweater. She's pulling it over her head, so the words are trapped in the knit as her head emerges. "If you can't get these first eight right, how are you going to learn more?"

I swallow the growl that wants to erupt and count to ten. See, I'm so good at counting to eight, I can add more to it.

"We can polish it after I've learned a chunk of it. If we wait until every piece is perfect before building on it, we won't have a whole dance. Unless the plan is to do the same eight counts twenty times."

Tiny fists get planted on shapely hips as she glares up at me. Her blonde hair is up in a ponytail, and her gray tank is molded to her high, firm breasts. but they look gorgeous with a slight sheen of sweat glistening on them. Wait, she's glaring, and that's usually not a sign of attraction. Focus, Trevor.

"Are you trying to tell me how to teach, Trevor?" Her Irish lilt gets more cutting when she's angry. Maybe it's the Scottish side of her coming out.

"No," I respond as calmly as I can. If we're both frustrated, I see this rehearsal going downhill quickly. I'll take one for the team and swallow my annoyance. "I'm trying to explain how I can learn."

She tosses her head, causing her ponytail to swish. It's a good thing she's short, otherwise I'd be getting thwapped in the face with it.

"I don't see the point in building on a faulty foundation."

The chuckle escapes before I'm even aware of it bubbling up.

She glares at me through narrowed blue eyes. "What's so funny?"

I hold up my hands in a "no offense" gesture. "I've heard Mac say the same thing, and it was funny hearing Mac's words in your voice. That's it. And like I've told him, progress is better than perfection. The dance is a minute and a half, right?"

She nods.

"Okay, so we need a ninety second dance in two weeks—"

"Ten days."

I nod. "Ten days. So, teach me the dance in three chunks over the next few days. Then we spend the next week or so polishing it."

Sophie's head is shaking so hard I'm afraid it's going to fall off.

"No! There's no point in learning new stuff when you don't know the old stuff. It's like trying to teach hockey to someone who doesn't know how to skate."

I know she thinks she's right, but she's not. At least, she's not right about the best way for me to learn this.

"Sometimes good enough is, well…good enough. It's better to have ninety seconds of something than ten seconds of perfection and standing there twiddling our thumbs for the other eighty seconds. Can't we at least try it this way, and if it doesn't work, we'll try your way next week?" I think that's a fair compromise.

Her sniff of disdain shows she does not. "We probably won't be there for week two if we do it half-assed like you're suggesting."

Now I'm getting pissed. "It's not half-assed. It's how I'll be able to learn the dance. I'm doing the best I can." I cross my arms over my chest. I took psychology in college. I know it's a defensive posture, but damn it, I'm feeling defensive. "If I'm spending all my time doing this, I want to win. I'm not going to suggest something that sabotages us. It's not like I asked for any of this. I was volun-told in front of a crowd."

Sophie huffs. "Well, you weren't my first choice, boyo, but I know Dec won't do it."

My brows lift at being called "boyo." I don't think it's a term of endearment.

"I still don't know how it's going to work to learn dance routines in addition to hockey practice and games," I say. Bitterness probably creeps into my voice. No matter how sexy the little blonde before me is, no matter how sweet her kisses, I should be on the ice, not dancing, dammit.

Her arms are crossed now too, but I'm not registering defensiveness. I'm distracted by the way her boobs are lifted and the top swells of her breasts are visible out of the neckline of her tank top.

"Fine," she snarls. "We'll do it your way. But you need to learn the whole thing in three days so we can spend the rest of the time polishing."

After the stress of this morning's rehearsal and having to endure Sophie's endless criticism when I'm trying my best, the last thing I want to do is spend the afternoon practicing *again* in the theater with Nigel and Nasty, I mean Nancy, watching and filming every little misstep I make.

I was able to get the basic steps down in our morning practice, but it took so long I didn't get any ice time to decompress before this afternoon's practice. I need to be on the ice. It's where I can let everything go. If I don't get it, I'm all keyed up and growly. We're filming where she starts "teaching" me the dance. That's why we busted our asses last night and this morning—so it would look like I was picking up the steps faster. Best foot forward and all that bullshit. I want to be in skates and slapping a puck into the net. Not talking about hip movements and flowy arms.

"Flirt!" Nancy snaps, waving her clipboard. "Sophie, bat those lashes and ask him if he's single. You know what's expected of you!"

They expect her to act like a simpering idiot?

"So, Trevor," Sophie says with a grin. "Are you single?"

Bat, bat, bat goes her eyelashes. Gone is the spunky woman from this morning with her ponytail and a fierce stubborn streak. This afternoon, Sophie's made up with false eyelashes and hair that looks sexily tousled but somehow still sporty. She's hot, but it's so fake it's leaving me cold. I'll play a role in this charade.

Turning on the charm, I grin. "That's how we're going to start? Okay. I am, Sophie. Are you?" At her nod, I turn up the sizzle in my smile. "That'll make dancing together all the more fun." We gaze into each other's eyes like we're seconds away from getting naked.

"Great!" Nancy says. Nigel rolls his eyes behind her. Sophie shuts off the coquettish sparkle like it's a faucet. If the dancing thing doesn't work out, she should pursue a career on the stage. She can act. I almost believed she was attracted to me for a moment, not merely tolerating me as a means to an end.

Nancy gestures for us to move to the center of the room. We're in one of the backstage studios in the theater. The winter afternoon sun is trying to bleed in through the windows, but it's a losing battle. The icy wind off the Atlantic Ocean is rattling the glass. It almost sounds like a cha-cha beat. "Show him the first few steps, Sophie."

Sophie does as directed, and I watch intently, then try them. Sophie and I discussed that I'm supposed to pretend this is new and make a minor mistake or two to start and then do the steps correctly.

We work our way through the first few sets of eight counts, and it's the smiling, supportive Sophie whose hand I'm holding now as we do side-by-side work across the floor. She's calling out counts, and I'm trying my best to dance to the rhythm of her counts—and now the beat of the windows. I can see the frustration flash in her eyes when I miss a step.

"Oops! Missed a step there, Trevor. Let's try again. You're doing a great job." To the world, it looks like she's smiling, but I know she's gritting her teeth and probably wants to smack me.

Mercifully, rehearsal ends, and we confirm when and where we're supposed to be for tomorrow's cast announcement. We're riding in Teagan Penhall's chopper. We'll leave at five in the morning and arrive in Manhattan an hour later. Allowing for traffic, we should be at the studio at half-past six for hair and makeup. The show's costume designers will be there, taking measurements while we're getting ready so they can start pulling basic costume pieces for us to wear during the promo shots we'll do after the cast announcement. There will be meetings with producers and other staff and interviews with stations around the country. It'll be a full day that will hopefully have us back home by dinnertime.

I'm going to miss hockey practice tomorrow. That's annoying. With Mac not playing and Crosby moved up, we need to get reps in so we're comfortably working with each other. Regardless of what I told Sophie, I do subscribe to the practice-makes-perfect philosophy with my hockey. I like to run plays until they're second nature. I like to know my wingers' habits so well I can just sense where they are on the ice and get the puck to them without looking. It's kind of like dancing. When you rehearse enough and know your partner, you can reach out your hand and be confident they're going to grasp it. That's how I am with my teammates. It would be nice if I could get there with Sophie, too.

6

SOPHIE

I'VE FLOWN IN PRIVATE PLANES BEFORE, BUT NEVER IN A PRIVATE HELICOPTER. Traveling in the predawn hours is breathtaking. The pinks and purples rising from the east are beautiful. It reminds me of the northern lights I've seen from my home in Scotland. Stunning. The rosy fingers of dawn stretching across the sky seem to beckon us to a new beginning. Hopefully it's a portent of good things to come for the show.

We land on the helipad on top of the studio building and take an elevator down to the hair and makeup room. Surprisingly, Trevor is not a morning person. He's not grumpy, just quiet. It's weird because he's usually such a large presence in any room, but it's nice having his silent strength next to me.

"You okay?" I ask from the makeup chair next to his. We're waiting our turn, and the hustle and bustle around us almost creates a little island of privacy.

He takes a sip of coffee and nods. "Yeah, just waking up. Don't worry, I'll be obnoxious in an hour or so once the caffeine hits." The way he gives me a half grin when he says that is adorable. It's just a quirk of the lips, one side slightly higher than the other, but it makes butterflies take flight in my belly.

I bump him with my shoulder. "You're not obnoxious, you're just...animated."

The throaty chuckle that washes over me like a warm shower doesn't help the butterflies settle down. It's crazy. I only spent one night in his arms, and I felt so lonely this morning getting up before dawn to make our flight and not having him there beside me. Not good, Sophie girl, not good.

"I won't let you forget you said that." He bumps my shoulder gently with his own.

"Good morning! Let's get you gorgeous!" A guy around our age comes up to us. His long black hair is half up in a ponytail, and the rest falls in a multicolored riot of teal, pink, and purple to his shoulders. "I'm Xavier. He/him." He holds out his hand for us to shake.

Trevor eyes him. Oh, please don't let him be homophobic because I will refuse to work with him, and I need this job. And our little fling we've got going on will be a no-go.

"Your hair is so cool," Trevor says with a touch of awe in his voice. My mouth drops. If someone asked me what I would expect this giant, manly hockey player to say, it would not be complimenting another man on his hair.

"Thanks, man!" Xavier says. "Check this out."

He removes the black hair tie creating the half pony, and his black hair falls in a solid curtain, hiding the multicolored pink, teal, and purple strands.

"Business mode," Xavier says. Trevor nods. "And party mode." Xavier quickly puts the top layer of his hair back up in the bun and flips the colorful strands over his shoulder.

Trevor looks at me. "Your hair would look pretty with that type of coloring. I don't have the patience to grow my hair out, and it's too wavy."

I tilt my head, trying to picture him with long hair. I can't do it. His brown hair is rich with copper tones. I think letting a drop of dye touch it would be a sin. Xavier agrees with me. Standing behind Trevor, he puts his hands on his shoulders and looks at him sternly in the mirror.

"Never, ever, dye your hair." He runs his fingers through it. "Women pay so much money trying to get hair with this depth of color and highlights. A picture of you could be in the hair books to use as an example of what they want. It's gorgeous."

A flush creeps up Trevor's cheeks. It's from being complimented, not from having a man running his fingers through his hair. I know a lot of men wouldn't be comfortable being touched like that. They aren't homophobic. They're just not used to touching other men outside of sports or roughhousing. I enjoy seeing this side of him.

"Thanks, that's kind of you. Oh, I'm Trevor Carter. He/him as well. And this is Sophie Mackenzie." He pats my arm.

I shake Xavier's hand. "Good morning. She/her." Every word I say somehow comes out awkward. Trevor isn't awkward at all. Impressive. It's lame that the bar to impress me is set so low. I should have higher standards for him.

"You're the pro, right?" Xavier asks.

I nod.

"And you play hockey, Trevor?"

"Yeah, for the Atlantic City Devil Birds. I play center."

Xavier laughs. "Oh, I know. My husband and I are huge hockey fans. We have Rangers season tickets and have been enjoying the PHL. You're a joy to watch play, killer wrist shot. Could I get your autograph for him?"

"Sure, I'd be happy to." He takes the pen and paper Xavier hands him. "What's their name?"

"Vincent."

Trevor writes something I can't see and hands the paper back to Xavier. He reads it before he tucks the slip of paper into his gear bag and gives a bark of laughter.

"What did you write?" I ask.

All I get in response is a sexy wink.

"Good morning, friends! Who's ready to get their shifter shimmy on?" Greta Knowles, the way-too-perky-this-early-in-the-morning show host, asks, smiling brightly at the camera.

Her morning show co-host Brandon Smiley—I don't know if I hope that's his real name or that he changed it for career reasons—wiggles his shoulders and beams. It's a cliché, but the set lights gleam off his blindingly white smile. I can almost hear a ping sound effect.

"I am, Greta!" Brandon says. "I can't wait to meet the contestants and pros for this season's *Celebrity Dance Dare*. It's a special shifter edition, so they'll be bringing their animal magnetism"—he does a lame-ass growl and swiping paw motion with his hand that tempts me to shift into my wolf and show him how to do it correctly—"to the dance floor along with their moves."

Trevor gives me the slightest of nudges with his elbow, and I do my best to look around casually so I can see the twitch of his lips betraying his amusement. The other pros and contestants roll their eyes or fight twitchy lips. Apparently everyone thinks Mr. Smiley's a prat.

We're lined up offstage, ready to be introduced one pair at a time as our names are

announced. There are eight teams in total, and we're fourth in line. Trevor is by far the most handsome of the men here.

Greta gives me the smile women everywhere recognize. The one we give when we're forced to work with a man less qualified than we are who probably makes twice our pay and we're still expected to be perky.

She gives a tinkling laugh that's more like shattering glass falling to the pavement than tinkling bells. "Yes, Brandon. Let's see who's competing for the Platinum Paw trophy. Our first pair is none other than charismatic actor Caleb Harkor and his pro partner, the sizzling salsa sensation Isabella Hernandez!"

The small studio audience erupts in applause as Caleb and Isabella make their entrance, showcasing their dance chemistry with a quick spin and a dazzling pose.

Brandon stares at the teleprompter, waiting for the studio intern to signal the audience to stop clapping. "Next up, we have the enchanting actress Olivia Mayes, paired with the king of smooth moves, Derek Duffy!"

Olivia and Derek glide onto the stage, radiating elegance and grace as they strike a pose. The excited crowd cheers.

The next team is announced, then it's our turn. Trevor squeezes our clasped hands. I don't know if it's to reassure me or himself. I squeeze his hand in return.

Brandon's grin is smarmy as he prepares to introduce us. "And now, from the boards to the ballroom, we bring you professional hockey player Trevor Carter and ballroom princess Sophie Mackenzie!"

We enter the stage doing side-by-side cha-cha steps that transition smoothly into me spinning into Trevor's arms and ending with a dramatic dip. I think the audience is clapping loudly, but it could be my blood pounding in my ears. Why did they have to introduce me like that?

"You okay?" Trevor murmurs as I go upright and smile brightly for the cameras. We aren't wearing microphones, but I know better than to assume there's any privacy in a studio.

"Mm-hmm."

We take our seats as the rest of the cast is introduced. I know some of the professional dancers from dancing with them on the UK and Irish versions of the show. Others I've competed against growing up. But I don't know the celebrities as well. They're mostly from American pop culture—some reality television types, former child stars, social media influencers, or aging film stars. Trevor is the only athlete.

When we've all been announced, we sit in a horseshoe shape with Greta and Brandon at the top. The three judges sit in front of our leg of the horseshoe, and there are two empty seats in front of the other leg. I assume that's for the *Celebrity Dance Dare* hosts. I've no idea who they'll be. The producers have kept their identities under wraps.

Greta flashes a warm smile and sweeps us with her gaze. "Raise your hand if you're a teensy bit nervous to be dancing on national TV!" Chuckles come from the cast and most of us raise our hands. So do a couple of the judges.

Carlo Estevez, the sassy Spanish judge wearing his signature mesh shirt and leather pants, puts his hand down. "You know it's bad when the pros are raising their hands too!"

Everyone laughs with him.

"We've been keeping a secret from everyone this season. Who's ready to meet our hosts?"

Applause sweeps through the audience and cast. There have been rumors of movie stars, pop princesses, and supermodels, but nothing definitive. The hosts really set the tone for the show, how they interact with each other and with the celebrities and pros. It's a delicate balance between a host who thinks they're the star and one working to present the contestants to their best advantage.

"Our first host has been where many of you are, competing for the Diamond Dance Shoe. While she didn't win her season, she won our hearts. Welcome, DeeDee Fowler!" Brandon stands, clapping as a gorgeous Black woman joins us. I covet her curve-hugging red wrap dress. She's a former model turned talk show host and I can tell she's going to be warm with the audience. DeeDee extricates herself from the hug Brandon holds too long. I hope the second host can keep up with her.

Greta gives DeeDee a much more appropriate hug and turns back to the camera. "Our second host is also familiar with the ballroom, but from the other side of the pond. While he'll be a new face to most of us, one of you knows him *very* well."

A wave of icy dread washes over me, causing me to shiver even though the studio lights are sweltering hot.

"Please welcome two-time pro dance champion of the British version of *Celebrity Dance Dare* and twin brother of our pro, Sophie, Ian Mackenzie!"

My training kicks in. I keep my smile firmly in place and clap with everyone else as Ian walks out. It's Greta's turn to give an inappropriately long hug. Ian is gorgeous. He's tall and lean with golden blond hair, blue eyes, and a brilliant smile. We shared a womb, and he got all the charm that was floating around while I got all the sass. At least, that's what our mother's told us since we were children.

He smiles and waves before walking over to me and giving me a hug. We're sitting in director's chairs, so he doesn't have to bend far to reach me and saves me from having to scramble down. He's in a bright blue suit that should look ridiculous, but on him, it looks elegant and classy. I feel dowdy in my flirty pink dress compared to my twin's tall elegance. I thought I looked cute next to Trevor in his light-blue button-down shirt with the sleeves rolled up to expose his muscular forearms and his tailored black slacks that hug his bum and thick thighs. It's not fair to be surrounded by gorgeous men all the time.

"Surprise!" he says as he pulls back. His smile falters. I'm sure I'm the only one who notices, and I feel guilty. I'm happy to see him and excited he's getting this great opportunity to do something beyond dancing. Thank goodness it's just hosting and not as a judge. No way could I escape claims of nepotism if he was handing out the scores. No matter how well we performed, the legitimacy of our scores would be questioned. It's just...I wish his opportunity didn't have to come at the expense of mine. I'm once again the second-best Mackenzie. Now, more than ever, I'll have to prove I'm good enough.

"What a surprise!" I cry. "I wasn't expecting to see you here!"

Trevor stands and shakes Ian's hand. Ian claps him on the shoulder. "You hit the jackpot, Trevor. You couldn't ask for a better partner than my baby sister."

Rolling my eyes as Ian takes his seat next to DeeDee, I clarify. "I'm two minutes younger than Ian."

Greta turns her attention to DeeDee and Ian. "We are so excited to have you two hosting."

"So excited," Brandon chimes in. "What makes you think you're the winning combo?"

DeeDee gives a huge smile. "Our personalities! We know what it's like to compete. To win and to lose. Ian is a sweetheart."

"And gorgeous!" Mary Ann Balboa, another of the judges, calls out.

"And talented," the third judge, Glen Woodman—the elder statesman of the ballroom and a dear friend of our mother's—says. "I've had the pleasure of watching Ian and Sophie dance through the years, as I have so many of the professional dancers, and it's more than being beautiful or handsome. More than the gorgeous costumes. There are years of hard work and sacrifice on display in the ballroom."

Ian is nodding. "Thank you, Glen. This season will be a lot of fun. It's all about letting the stars shine brightly." He grins sheepishly, reminding me of the boy I knew. "Excuse the cliché."

We all chuckle.

"Yes!" DeeDee gives Ian a high five.

"Carlo," Greta crosses her legs, "what are the judges hoping to see this season?"

That's all it takes for Carlo to jump out of his seat and start gesturing madly.

"We want to see fabulous dancing, passion." His gaze is on me and Trevor as if he expects that passion from us, but maybe I'm imagining that. "Most of all, we want to see everyone having fun. Yes, technical perfection is a goal, but life is short. Enjoy every moment of it."

"Perfectly said, Carlo," Brandon gushes with what I think he thinks is a sincere expression. This guy is so smarmy. I want to take a shower after being in his presence. As much as Ian being a host is a shock, I'm glad it's not someone like Brandon. I know my brother will be kind and respectful. Trevor nudges my foot with his. I can hear the whoosh of breath with a hint of an "ugh" in it. It's not only microphones we have to worry about catching what we say, we're in a room full of shifters who can hear and see everything. We'll practically have to read each other's minds if we want to communicate without everyone knowing our business.

Our segment is over, and everyone's backstage in the green room chatting and getting to know each other. I'm off to the side, like I usually am with crowds. It's not that I'm shy, it's just mentally overwhelming being around so many people with elevated emotions. People tease Declan about reading their minds. He can't, but like me, he's an empath. We're observant and deeply feel the surrounding vibrations. Unlike Declan, I have to keep a shield around me to survive. My feelings are too tender. It makes me seem like an unfeeling bitch, and that hurts. I don't know how to balance protecting myself and being open.

Ian brings me a bottle of water that I accept gratefully.

"I'm sorry I couldn't tell you about the hosting gig. Ma didn't know either. Are you okay with it?" He's speaking quietly and in a deep brogue that won't be easily understood by the casual listener.

"I'm happy for you. You know that. It will be nice to see each other every week."

He hears everything I didn't say. "We'll talk about it later?"

"Aye."

"So, Declan and Miranda?"

I sigh. "Aye."

"Did we see that coming?" he asks.

"I didn't," I admit. "Did you?"

He shrugs and takes a sip of his orange juice. "He's had a crush on her forever, but I didn't know she felt the same way."

Trevor joins us and hands me a chocolate donut. This is one of the things I like about America—chocolate donuts with brightly colored nonpareils on them. He calls them jimmies. I call them yummy and fun.

"They're perfect for each other," Trevor says.

Ian's brow furrows like he doesn't quite believe Trevor.

But Trevor's unmovable in his certainty. "I've known Randi for six years. She's one of my best friends. He's my teammate. They live with me. He's exactly the type of man I'd want for her."

"Really?" Ian asks.

"We have a ton to catch up on, Ian," I say. "But it looks like it's time to get measured, so it'll have to be another time."

Costume fitters enter the green room and zero in on me and Trevor. I quickly finish eating my donut before they join us.

I stretch up to give Ian a kiss on the cheek. "We'll catch up soon. Love you."

His strong arm curves around me in a quick hug while his other reaches out to shake Trevor's. "Love you too, Soph. Good luck, Trevor, with the dancing but also with this spitfire."

"Thanks, Ian. It's been great meeting you. Luck is already on my side, getting Sophie as my partner. I wouldn't want to do this without her."

I'm touched. And scared. I can't let these feelings slip past my shield. While I'm willing to dance my heart out, I refuse to put it on a platter to be broken.

7

TREVOR

"THEY REALLY LIKE TO GET UP CLOSE AND PERSONAL MEASURING FOR THE costumes, don't they?" I ask as I drive us from the airport back to Devil's Den. It's midafternoon, and we've been to New York City and back. I could learn to really enjoy traveling like this. No catching a bus from one of the casinos or taking a patchwork of trains to avoid having to drive in the city and find parking.

Sophie giggles. "They want to show you off to your best advantage…and make sure you don't split a seam."

Shuddering, I grip the wheel tighter. "Don't even joke about that. I had that happen once on the sideline of a football game. I squatted to prepare to lift Randi, and as she went up in the air, I felt a cool breeze on my twig and berries. My arms were fully extended above my head, keeping Miranda in the air as she did the cheer and stunts, so I couldn't cover up. I gave a stadium full of people a show."

"Oh, no, wardrobe malfunctions are the worst! They measure the female dancers to the millimeter, and we're taped and glued six ways to Sunday to ward off nip slips or flashing the kitty." Sophie makes a *yikes* face, and it's my turn to chuckle. Wardrobe malfunctions are the nightmares of people in the public eye everywhere. "What did you do? Other than pose proudly and let the world bask in your glory?"

"How did you know that's what I named him?" I deadpan, earning a spluttering laugh from Sophie as she backhands me in the bicep. "Got through the routine, and as soon as Randi was safely on the ground, I grabbed her pom-poms to cover my package and rushed back to the locker room for another pair of pants. I was getting more cheers than the football team." The memory, though mortifying, makes me smile. Even though I was wearing compression briefs, I was still looking good enough to get some extra female attention after the fact. I was in my second year of law school, so there were lots of jokes about my briefs.

She adjusts in her seat so she can face me better.

"Why were you a cheerleader? Why didn't you play football? I'm sure you could've if you wanted."

My shoulders stiffen. I've heard this question so many times, but I didn't expect it from her.

"Why does your brother dance? Why do you dance? To dance the way you do, you have skills that could be used for gymnastics or martial arts. I cheered because I enjoy moving. I like using my strength." I flash what I'm told is my panty-melter grin. "And there were no girls on the football team."

"Ugh." She groans and punches me in the arm. "That's gross."

I lean away to try to get out of her reach, but that's the problem with driving a sports car and not an SUV. Nowhere to hide.

"I'm being honest! They needed guys, and I got a scholarship. I was able to save money for law school. My family is comfortable, but they aren't wealthy. I had some parental support for school, but I was expected to take out loans and work. Law school is expensive." She nods in understanding. "I got a good enough scholarship for cheer that I didn't have to take out loans for the last two years of undergrad. It made my law school applications interesting, and since I attended Wickham, I could cheer for two more years and get more scholarship money to use for law school. Obviously, my loans were the first thing I paid off when I got money from playing hockey. Then I bought my baby." I pat the dashboard of my BMW affectionately.

I stop at the light in the middle of the outlet store complex. Even on a frigid January day like this, shoppers are rushing from store to store, taking advantage of post-holiday sales.

"Do you plan on practicing law when you're done playing hockey, or will you go into coaching?" she asks.

I guess she doesn't know the plan Randi and I originally had for our careers.

"Well, before the PHL was announced and it became possible to play professional hockey, I was planning on being a sports agent. I love sports more than I love law, but having a law degree is necessary to be the type of agent I want to be. I have no plans to ever set foot in a courtroom, it's all contracts and endorsement deals for me. Randi and I were going to work together. She majored in sports manage-ment, and our plan was to represent professional athletes. When the PHL was announced and I decided to go that way, she decided to go to New Zealand after she graduated from Wickham. I still want to be an agent when I'm done playing, but I think Randi's plans have changed. We'll see." I pull into the garage for Devil's Den and take my usual spot.

"You're coming in?" Sophie asks, undoing her seat belt.

I hit the button to pop the trunk. "No, I'm going over to The Nest to skate and run some drills, and then there's the junior team prac-tice. I try to attend them when I can."

She follows me to the rear of my car as I get my gear bag out. "Junior team?"

We exit the garage and hurry across the Boardwalk to The Nest. The wind is icy. I'm glad we went to New York before the moisture in the air had the chance to become snow or freezing rain.

"Yeah, we have a few teams for kids in the community to learn hockey and play competitively. Different age groups. My nephews play. I enjoy working with the kids. Most of the players help when our schedules allow us." I consider it one of the better things about my job, but I'm not going to admit that.

Sophie rushes through the door I hold open for her, eager to get out of the cold. She brushes against me lightly, and a zing runs through me. It must be static electricity built up in her navy-blue wool peacoat. I'm not a scientist like Bedard is, but I'm willing to experiment to see if we could build up a static charge rubbing against each other. Naked. In bed. For sure there will be sparks of some kind. I can't wait for this fling we keep talking about to stop being a topic of conversation and start being a verb. Like me flinging her clothes to the floor. Me flinging her onto the bed. Her flinging her hair over her shoulders as she rides my cock. Less talking, more flinging.

"You like kids?" An odd expression flits across her face, and my thoughts of flings come to a screeching halt. Flings and talk of kids do not belong together.

Shrugging, I turn toward the practice rinks. I can hear sticks striking pucks and assume some of my teammates had the same idea of getting in some informal ice time.

"Yeah, I do. They're fun, honest, and let you know where you stand. I enjoy teaching them and seeing their excitement when they learn a new skill." And I can give them back after practice. Kids are great, but not being responsible for keeping them alive and happy is even better.

I think she's going to say something, but Stone calls out from the door to the first practice rink.

"Hey there, twinkle toes, how did it go? Watched the announcement online." He turns to Sophie. "Your brother as a host is a plot twist, huh?"

Stone loves to read, so half of his statements have to do with books. I don't think he even realizes it.

"Aye, wasn't expecting that. But that's how these shows are, always throwing in twists and turns. There's a fine line between being comfortable and predictable. Predictability is the kiss of death for reality television."

Stone nods, kinda looking like a bearded bobblehead, as he steps aside for us to enter the rink. "Hmm...yeah. But you probably wanted a chance to do this on your own, right? Working with family is hard."

Sophie stumbles slightly. My hand shoots out on instinct to steady her. Heat floods her cheeks.

"Do you think being on the team and living with your sister is hard?" she asks. Stone's sister Bridget is our star goalie. She's nicknamed Brick because their last name is Waller and she's like a brick wall blocking the goal.

I head to the benches alongside the boards so I can put my skates on. Sophie sits next to me, and Stone leans against the boards, facing us.

His mouth quirks to the side as he rubs his thick beard. That's something I like about him. He thinks before he speaks. He's goofy as hell and a fun guy to hang out with, but he's the type of man that, when he says something, you listen.

"I think Bridget and I being on the same team is different than you and your brother. Yeah, we play the same sport, but in completely different roles. Our destinies and success weren't intertwined. You and Ian were partners, right? And then he got a new one, and you didn't? He got a pro spot, and you didn't." He looks sheepish. Moose-ish? "I Googled. I'm a curious person with excellent research skills. No offense intended."

Sophie huffs out a laugh. "None taken! I appreciate your candor." She looks out over the practice ice where some of my teammates are skating. She adjusts her position on the bench. The practice rink at ice level doesn't have very comfortable seating.

"It's hard," she admits. "I love Ian. He's my twin. But I wanted this show to just be mine. Our careers have been so intertwined, like you said. And our mother is a big deal in the dance world too. I'm always an afterthought." The flush on her cheeks deepens. "I want to be the Mackenzie in the spotlight. Just me. Because of what I've accomplished. Not something that people can say my mother or my brother helped me achieve."

To lighten the mood, I bump Sophie's shoulder with my own as I lace up my skates.

"You need me though, princess."

She bumps me back. "I do, boyo. Don't screw this up for me."

Something wicked causes me to lean in and breathe into Sophie's ear. "If there's screwing between us, it's not on the dance floor."

Stone is looking everywhere but at us. I don't know if moose shifters have the extra sensitive hearing that wolf shifters like me and Sophie do, but I trust he'll pretend to have no clue.

"Oof." The breath whooshes out of me when Sophie jams her elbow into my ribs. For never playing hockey, she's mastered throwing elbows and body checks.

"Do you skate, Sophie?" Stone asks. "There's a rental skate counter so we can get you a pair."

Sophie shakes her head vehemently. "No. I can't skate, and I can't risk getting injured trying to learn how. I could invalidate my contract with the show if I was injured doing something risky like that and couldn't perform. I'm not allowed to go horseback riding, skiing, or skydiving either. Not that there was any risk of me doing those things, anyway."

"You don't ride?" I ask.

"I don't like horses. They're big and smelly. I know Declan and Miranda are gaga for them, but not me. Even though I'm a shifter, I'm not really an animal person. I don't kick puppies or anything, but I'm not into things crawling on me or licking me."

My wiggling brows make her flush scarlet and Stone choke on a laugh. I shouldn't be flirting with her like this, but I can't help it.

She gestures toward the ice. "Go skate. Do your thing."

"Are you staying?" I ask.

"For a bit, but then I'll go back to my room. I'm exhausted. I don't know how you have the energy to skate."

Winking, I give my panty-melting smile. "I'm known for my stamina."

Stone wrinkles his nose. "All righty. This has been fun. I'll leave you two to do your thing."

"We're not doing anything!" Sophie calls after him as he steps onto the ice.

I get to my feet and prepare to follow him, but hold back and lower my voice, leaning in close enough to Sophie that I can smell her strawberry scent. "Not this very moment, we're not. But we're about due to consummate our fling, don't you think, princess?" I wink and drop my gaze to her perfect lips. "Your place or mine tonight? Text me." I skate away, feeling her pull like a magnet. I skate faster to break it. This fling is temporary. I can't give her forever.

8

SOPHIE

I watch Trevor skate with his teammates for a few minutes and record him. I think I can adapt some of the plays they run into dance moves.

"Hey, wasn't expecting to see you here," Miranda says as she sits next to me. My brother and Bedard are joining the others on the ice.

"We finished in New York early," I say, "and Teagan is letting us use her helicopter, so it's only about an hour getting back here. We're being incredibly spoiled."

Miranda nods. "You should be spoiled. Trev being on *Celebrity Dance Dare* is a tremendous marketing opportunity for the Devil Birds and the PHL. All the dance practice plus the travel and playing hockey is going to be exhausting. For both of you. Take advantage of any perks you can to preserve your energy."

The noise in the rink increases as kids arrive with their parents.

"Let's go up in the stands so the kids can use the benches to get their skates on."

I follow her up a few rows and settle in a pair of seats at center ice. The practice rink is a full-sized sheet of ice but doesn't have as much seating as the main rink, so we can all see the action. Local schools and recreation leagues use this rink for their games and practices.

"I have grown-up hot cocoa," Miranda says, holding up a thermos. "Want some?"

That sounds intriguing and slightly inappropriate for a kids' hockey practice. Totally my sort of thing.

"Sure," I say. "What makes it grown-up?"

"Peppermint schnapps. For you, it'll just be flavoring, not enough to make you tipsy. It won't even make me tipsy. But it makes these practices more fun."

Shrugging, I nod. She reaches into her bag and pulls out a big thermos and two cups. Just then, Kendall plops into the seat next to Miranda.

"Ooh, just in time for cocoa! I have the cookies." She pulls a bakery box out of her bag. I feel less silly about the random stuff I carry, like dance shoes, tights, and dance clothes. "The pink dress you were wearing, is that yours?"

I nod.

"Where did you get it? I think we're about the same size."

Miranda snorts as she grabs more cups out of her bag, hands them to Kendall, and starts pouring. "Same size? You're practically twins! You both have blond hair and blue eyes. Tiny. I'd believe Kendall's your sister before thinking Declan is your brother."

She hands one to me. "That's for Mallory."

That's when I notice Mallory on my other side. I was so focused on the cocoa commotion that I didn't register someone sitting inches away from me. *Thanks for looking out for me*, I tell my wolf. She just curls into a tighter ball and plops her tail over her eyes. My shifter is firmly in decorative mode, no function to be found. Awesome.

I hand Mallory the cup Miranda poured.

"Thanks!" she says, pushing her coppery hair over her shoulder with the hand not holding the cocoa. She and Trevor have similar coloring, but Mallory's is morevibrant. Her hair is redder; her eyes are green to his hazel. They are both outgoing. "I saw you and Trev on the morning show. You looked great! Did you know your brother was going to be a host?"

"Oh, yeah," Daphne says from the other side of Mallory, "you looked shocked. Had it been a secret, or are you that good of an actress?"

Before I can say anything, Miranda hands me another cup of cocoa. "That's for Daphne. No booze."

"Thanks, sweetie!" Daphne leans back to say. Her hand is resting on her belly, rubbing soothing circles. Daphne is adorable, but she's loud. In a happy way. But it's still a lot. Birdie is probably going to be able to sleep through anything. Birdie is the nickname they have for the baby since Logan is a golden eagle shifter. They don't know if they are having a boy or girl yet so Birdie is their default name for their child for now.

I accept my cup from Miranda and take a cautious sip. It's warm but not scalding hot. We can drink it right away. I taste the peppermint, and while I always think my family's whisky is the proper choice for alcohol, this is refreshing.

Remembering Daphne asked me a question, I swallow my cocoa and answer. "Total surprise. I assumed he was enjoying the hiatus before his show starts again in May. He never told me he was interested in hosting. I thought his plan was to dance and maybe eventually become a judge like our mother."

"Are all of your brothers gorgeous?" Mallory asks.

Before I can answer, Miranda shouts, "Yes!"

I eye her cup. Did she add extra schnapps to hers? She's usually so soft-spoken that her outburst takes me by surprise. Maybe she needs to stick to the plain cocoa Daphne's drinking. I sink down in my seat to hide from the parents who glance up at us.

Miranda just waves. "Declan is the most handsome, of course, but they're all gorgeous."

"Are they all single?" Mallory asks. "I have an older sister I wouldn't mind shipping off to the other side of the Atlantic some days."

"The twins, Patrick and Owen, are," I say. "They're a year older than I am. My younger brother, Seamus, has a girlfriend, but I'm not sure how serious it is. My twin, Ian, has a partner, Peter. He's a dancer on the show too. They've been together for almost two years."

"Does it bother you?" Kendall asks.

I'm shocked she'd ask something so rude. "No," I say frostily. "My brother is happy, and Peter is wonderful. Love is love."

Kendall blinks a few times and then shakes her head. "No! Oh my god, I'm sorry. I meant, does it bother you he's going to be on the show? My cousin Andy and his fiancé Harrison are my next-door neighbors and close friends. I'm absolutely with you on the love is love train."

I relax, slightly embarrassed I jumped to the conclusion I did. I'm protective of Ian. Not that being a gay man in the ballroom dance scene is unusual, but growing up, there were a lot of teasing and snide remarks. No one would say it to his face because of who our mother is. Being a massive wolf shifter probably helped keep lips zipped too. But that didn't stop them from gossiping where I could hear it. When I'd get upset, Ian would just laugh and say they were jealous he was a better dancer and more fabulous than they were. And that he wouldn't hook up with them. He was way better at recognizing predatory sleazes for who they were than I was.

After Ian and I stopped dancing together, I thought I was in love with an older man who claimed he wanted to be my partner on and off the floor. Turns out he just wanted another notch on his bedpost and the opportunity to be close to my mother in hopes of being tapped for a pro spot on the show. I wish I could say I only fell for that scheme once, but younger-me was a slow learner, and it took me two more times to realize they weren't in love with me. They wanted the connections and advantages being with me brought. Now when I hook up, I know that's all it is. Mutual pleasure, no promises, no future. I can't give them what they want anyway, so why pretend?

I haven't been with anyone in over a year. Dance has been my focus. I have toys to take care of my physical needs, and I have physical contact with my dance partners. That's enough. Most of the time. Of course, there's my fling with Trevor. A fling that has been annoyingly sparse.

Mallory gestures toward the ice with her cocoa cup. "Those two talking to Stone are my nephews," she says, inclining her head to two dark-haired little boys near the entrance to the rink.

As the kids get ready to take the ice, a little girl with red braids turns and waves wildly. "Hi, Miss Morgan!"

Kendall waves back. "Hi, Rowena!"

Rowena buckles the chin strap on her helmet and skates across the ice to Bedard.

Daphne chuckles. "She has such a crush on him. It's adorable."

"It's a mutual admiration society. He's a fan of hers, too." Kendall leans forward to speak to me. "I'm a first-grade teacher, and Rowena is one of my students. Burke volunteers at my school, so all the kids know him."

"Trevor always has a crowd. He's so good with kids," Mallory says.

Miranda nods. "He's going to have a whole pack." She turns to Kendall and bounces in her seat with excitement. "I love that my kids will get to grow up with your kids and Trevor's."

Kendall huffs out a laugh. "Slow your roll, Randi. I'm not getting remarried anytime soon, and single motherhood is *not* in my game plan. And Trevor isn't even dating anyone!"

Miranda turns a hopeful gaze my way.

I raise my hands like I'm going to ward off her questions, but no such luck.

"Don't look at me! We're dance partners, that's it. I'm not having a pack. I'm not having kids at all."

My eyes remained fixed on the kids skating. They're doing a drill where they pass pucks back and forth and then shoot at the goal. I can feel the weight of everyone's eyes on me. I'm a female wolf shifter. I'm supposed to want a big family. It's how it's done.

I'm unnatural.

No one is saying anything. Have I shocked them? Cautiously, I turn my head slightly to gauge Miranda's reaction. She's eating a chocolate chip cookie.

"What?" she mumbles while chewing.

I feel Mallory's touch on my forearm and turn toward her. "It's okay. I know the pressure female wolf shifters have to have big families, even now. I don't shift, but I still hear it. My sister doesn't want kids either. My mother only planned on having two—they were so exhausted with two kids they forgot they had sex after my sister was born, so Mom was shocked to discover she was four months pregnant five months after having my sister. Trevor was an oops. But Mom still thinks we should want five or six kids each. Liam and I only plan to have two. My older brother has two. Trevor will probably be the only one of us with a bunch of kids."

Well, that keeps Trevor firmly in the *only a fling* category. No strings, no future, no kids. We're having fun while we're together, and then when the show ends, we move on. He may end up with a ton of kids, but he knows they aren't coming from me.

We drink cocoa, chat about random things, and watch the practice for a while, but the exhaustion from the early morning trip to New York creeps up on me. Stifling a yawn, I snag a cookie to take with me and stand.

"It was lovely chatting with you all, but I need to get back to my room. I'm about to drop, and I need to pack for the two away games this week."

Not counting the All-Star Game, this will be my first time traveling with the team and working around their game-day schedule. We'll need to fit rehearsals wherever and whenever possible. We're not going to have a studio or a theater space. It will be hallways in arenas and hotel rooms. Trevor seems to be the type to be okay with challenging circumstances—hopefully he can adapt.

After everyone says goodbye, I walk down the stands to ice level so I can leave. I'm at the last step when Trevor skates up to the glass and motions me over. We move along to the bench area so we can talk without the glass separating us.

"Thanks for staying," Trevor says.

Shrugging, I gesture to Miranda with a jerk of my head. "There was spiked cocoa and cookies. Couldn't miss that."

If anyone ever asked, I'd insist it was the boozy cocoa making my stomach flutter and not Trevor's lopsided grin. I'd be lying.

"Are you going back to your room?"

"Yeah, I'm exhausted and need to pack for the road trip."

"What are you doing for dinner?" he asks.

"Ordering room service, probably. I need to catch up on sleep."

"Yeah, me too," he admits.

We stand there, looking at each other while kids zoom around laughing, the swoosh of their skate blades almost sounding like brushing a snare drum. The indistinct murmurs of their parents' conversations create a base-level hum that's punctuated by whistle blows starting and stopping drills. There's a rhythm and cadence to it that would be cool to sample into a track for a dance. I'll have to record it the next time I'm here and talk to the show's band leader to see if it's something we can use.

Slow grins spread across our faces as if we choreographed it. "See you in an hour?" I ask.

"Sooner if I can manage it," Trevor says with a wink.

"Shall I order dinner?"

His chuckle is low, and it makes my belly do funny things that I can't blame for the boozy cocoa.

"We can order...after," he says.

Heat rushes to my cheeks and other parts. Nodding, I turn and sashay away, knowing his eyes are on me.

As I leave The Nest and brave the icy wind blowing off the Atlantic to cross the Boardwalk to Devil's Den, I wonder if I should order sandwiches or something. With what I have in mind, there may not be an after. We may not end up getting any sleep at all once we're in a bed together again. I don't want to waste the night sleeping.

Jab. Jab. Jabbity jab jab. I keep pressing the button on the elevator like that will make it arrive faster. I'm eager to get to my hotel room so I can quickly pack and be free to enjoy the night with Trevor. When the door slides open, I step back quickly to allow the passengers off and then enter the car. Thankfully, I'm the only one on board, so I get to my floor quickly. Letting myself into the suite, I call down to order a selection of sandwiches along with a cheese plate and wine, so we can graze during the evening and not leave the room. Then, I hurriedly pack the essentials for our trip. If I forget anything, I'm sure I can either borrow it from Miranda or buy it at a local store.

I don't know whether to change into something sexier or stay as I am. Take a shower? I hate being uncertain. Before I can dither any further, there's a knock on my door. Rushing over, I open it to find Trevor standing there gorgeously rumpled, like he jumped off the ice and rushed over here. Which I guess he did. Because a quick glance shows I only left the rink thirty minutes ago.

"Hey," he says. stepping toward me.

"Hey, yourself," I respond, placing a hand on his jacket-covered chest and going on tiptoe to press a kiss on his jaw.

Dropping my heels to the floor, I undo his jacket. The man has way too many layers on. He helps by shrugging off his jacket and throwing it on the chair as he kicks the door closed. He wraps an arm around my waist, pulling me against him as he lowers his head to kiss me. His lips are firm but gentle. It's a sip of a kiss. His free hand comes up to rest against my cheek as his thumb gently caresses my face. This is new. This gentleness. I like it. But not right now. We can be gentle later. Right now, I want this man. Fiercely.

My hands skate up his chest and behind his neck to allow my fingers to burrow into his thick hair. As I increase the pressure of our lips, I nip at his bottom lip. He growls low in his throat. That growl ripples through me, igniting flames of desire. On impulse, I leap up and wrap my legs around his trim hips. Like a perfect dance partner, he reacts immediately and catches me, his large hands gripping my ass. I grind against him, feeling his desire for me. Yeah. It's about time this fling gets flung. A knock on the door breaks through the desire-laced fog our kisses enveloped us in. Reluctantly, I break away. Trevor groans in frustration.

"I think that's our food," I say, unwrapping my legs so he can lower me back to the floor.

"You can leave it by the door," Trevor calls out. "Thank you."

His hands are still on my ass, and he squeezes as he lowers his head to resume our kiss.

There's knocking again. "Sophie?" a deep voice calls. It's my brother. Damn it.

"I think Trevor's in there with her." That's Miranda. "We should go, Declan."

Yes, you should both go. Now.

I look up at Trevor with wide eyes. In silence, we acknowledge they know we're in here. Before I can say anything. I hear Declan say, "Oh. Hello. Yes, we'll take the sandwiches. We're joining them for dinner. Thank you so much."

Trevor sighs and his shoulders slump. There's no getting rid of them now. My brother will just camp outside the door and make a picnic of our dinner.

"We know you're in there, and we have your food. Open the damn door," Declan says in a sing-song voice at odds with his words.

With a sigh of my own, I step out of Trevor's arms and stomp over to the door, throwing it open. My eldest brother is standing there with a room service cart next to him and a shit-eating grin on his face.

"Are you going to invite us in? This looks like it would be plenty for the four of us."

Miranda mouths the word *sorry* as I step aside so Declan can wheel the cart in.

"Are we interrupting something?" Declan's tone is innocent, but his smirk isn't.

Trevor runs a hand through his hair, looking sheepish.

"Yes, you are," I say.

Declan chuckles. "Good. That makes up for you bursting in on us New Year's morning."

With a flourish, he removes the lid from the tray of sandwiches and grabs a ham and cheese, making himself at home on the sofa while reaching for the remote to turn on a hockey game.

I'm being cockblocked. By my brother. FML. Because nothing else is getting fucked tonight.

9
TREVOR

I'M TOO TIRED TO BE NERVOUS ABOUT PERFORMING ON THE FIRST EPISODE OF the shifter edition of *Celebrity Dance Dare* tonight. We had a two-game road trip to the Midwest where we beat Cincinnati but lost in Milwaukee. Out of the three games at home, we only won the second one. I hate losing.

I won't lose tonight.

I've got too many losses to make up for—on the ice and in the bedroom. Wasn't I supposed to be having a fling? Yes. But the universe seems to be against me. Cockblocked by my teammate, then cockblocked by Sophie's and my schedules. If one more thing cock-blocks me, I might just throw Sophie over my shoulder and lock her in my bedroom until...well, I don't know how long, but I want the time and space to savor Sophie's delectable body. I mean, we could have had quickies but that's not what I want for our first time together.

"You okay?" Sophie asks. She's next to me in her gold sequin-covered costume. I can't call it a dress. It's straps, mesh fabric that covers her but gives the illusion of nudity, and fringe. She's covered, but it's very sexy and flirty. I'm fully dressed in a black button-down with rolled-up sleeves to show off cream-colored cuffs that match the black pants with wide cream stripes down the outside seam of each leg.

"Yeah. Excited." The announcer is about to start the show. We rehearsed the introductions during the dress rehearsal we had earlier this afternoon. Big smiles, some shimmying, not passing out from nerves. First, Sophie joins in the group dance with the other pros, then joins me for our introduction.

Ian stands next to the judges' table, looking elegant in a gray suit with a red tie. "First up tonight is the Atlantic City Devil Birds' center, Trevor Carter, and his partner, Sophie Mackenzie, dancing the cha-cha."

We take our opening positions. I'm at the bottom of the steps on the stage and Sophie is posed in front of the judges' table. Ian gives his sister a wink, and it makes me smile. We didn't talk much today, but I can see how supportive and proud he is of his twin.

The music starts, and my heart pounds in time to the beat. Sophie struts across the floor and I watch her like she's prey enticing the predator in me. Her swinging hips make the fringe pretending to be a skirt swish back and forth. I follow her because my instinct says I must. Thankfully, the choreography agrees. The dance is a blur of steps and turns. Sophie is saying the counts as we go, and I hope I'm on beat and doing the correct moves. Her long blond hair is in a high ponytail, and it whips around as she spins. She grins, and it's not fake. It's her happy-Sophie smile, and it jolts something in me. I'm not in front of a crowd anymore. I'm alone in a studio. Just my princess and me, and we're dancing in a way that suggests it's foreplay. My limbs move easier than before, and I smile, too. For her. For us having fun. I relish every touch and anticipate with sweet desire every move that brings her hot body up against my own. I inhale against her neck and call her back with my eyes when she moves too far away from me. I'm seducing her with winks and grins and touches, and she's seducing me right back. And when the music takes its final leap into the air and she crouches in front of me provocatively, her head turned to look over her shoulder so she can wink at the camera behind her, I want to go full caveman and throw her over my shoulder, find the nearest private room and continue this fling we never quite started. But the audience is on their feet, yelling and clapping, and damn it, we're not alone. So I smile, and Sophie leaps into my arms.

And I try to tame the hard-on fighting against my dance cup. Thank goodness she didn't stay down there. That wink started blood flowing to places that I'm not sure the dance belt I'm wearing is prepared to contain. I return her hug and kiss her cheek. She's beautiful, with her blue eyes shining brightly, not just from the studio lights, but from happiness too. Her smile is radiant. Sophie's dream is coming true, and I'm thrilled to be a part of it. I wish I could be part of more, but I know I can't be.

We walk to where Ian is standing by the judges' table. Sophie is so excited, she's almost skipping. I follow close behind her. I want to rest my hand on the small of her back, but all that bare skin is a temptation I know I should resist.

Slipping his arm around Sophie's shoulders to give her a quick squeeze, Ian says, "What a way to open the show! How does it feel to make your debut as a pro partner, Sophie?"

"Incredible," she enthuses. "This is something I've dreamed of for so long. And I couldn't imagine doing it with anyone other than Trevor." She slides out from under Ian's arm and wraps her arms around my waist to hug me. Grinning, I return her hug as we give our attention to the judges and prepare to hear their opinions on our performance.

"Let's start with our head judge, Glen Woodman," Ian says. "Glen, what did you think?"

"Well, Ian, some couples are going to have blue skies. Others are going to experience lots of turbulence. Trevor and Sophie, get ready to soar in the friendly skies!" Glen smiles broadly, and the audience applauds loudly. I can see some of my teammates in the crowd. "But you need to dance tall, Trevor. I know there's a height difference, but don't dance down to her level. She's the pro, she will dance up to yours. Trust your partner."

Carlo stands, as he always does when giving feedback, and leans with both hands on the table. His black mesh shirt is see-through, and his leather pants are tight. Maybe he needs the mesh to balance the heat trapped by wearing leather under the studio lights.

"Trevor and Sophie," he says in his suave Spanish accent. "One of the secrets of the cha-cha is to come out and have fun. You looked like you were having fun! That was sizzling hot. Muy caliente. You're a very attractive couple." Carlo flutters his eyelashes coquettishly. "Trevor, you're a flirty one, aren't you?"

I give what I'm told is my boyish grin and shrug. "I may have been told that a time or two. I think I'm just being friendly, though." I punctuate that with a wink.

Carlo chuckles and wiggles his eyebrows suggestively. "I bet you have lots of friends. No doubt after tonight's performance, you will have many more people wanting to be your friend."

"Down, Carlo," Mary Ann scolds. She motions with a scarlet-tipped finger toward Carlo. "Can we get someone to wipe up the drool from the table?" The audience laughs, and when it dies down, she gives her critique. "Trevor, I think you have a lot of potential. You're not only a star on the ice, but I can see you being a star in the ballroom. The two of you have crazy chemistry. I can't wait to see what you bring to the dance floor. So nimble, the timing was excellent. You have natural performance power. But like Glen said, you're leaning forward. I know she's gorgeous, but you need to dance with her. Don't just grab her."

The audience boos.

"Stop," she chides. "We're here to help them get better. If they don't hear what the problems are, they won't be able to fix them and improve. This isn't criticism, it's critique. There's a difference."

Sophie and I nod. She's told me about using my full height, but with the size difference, I feel disconnected from her. I didn't realize it was noticeable, but Mary Ann is some sort of eagle shifter, so she's not going to miss a thing.

It's time for the judges to announce their scores. Mary Ann gives us a seven. Glen shocks everyone by scoring us an eight. Carlo waves his paddle bearing a seven. That adds up to a total of twenty-two points out of thirty. From watching past seasons of the show, I know that's a strong week one score. Especially for the first pair dancing for the night. That should have us toward the top of the scoreboard. Hopefully, the audience at home votes for us too. We thank the judges and head to the interview area where DeeDee waits for us.

"Way to open the show and the season! Great job! And that sizzling chemistry." She whips out a folding fan and waves it in front of her. "Is it hot in here, or is it you two? What do you think was your secret for working so well together this week?"

Sophie and I look at each other, and I motion for her to answer.

"Lots and lots of practice," she says. "Trevor's in the middle of his hockey season, so I'm traveling with the team to their away games. We're practicing in the hallway outside of locker rooms, in airports waiting to get on the plane, in hotel rooms. We're grabbing every moment we can to practice, and I'm shocked Trevor hasn't dropped yet. He's giving it his all with the dancing, plus playing multiple games of hockey each week, which is very physically demanding." She looks up at me and gives a quick smile. "Hockey is a contact sport. He's getting hit and knocked down. Fighting for the puck. Contending with bumps, bruises, and strains, and still practicing dance with me and giving his all just like he does on the ice. I don't know how he's doing it, but I couldn't ask for a better partner."

They both look at me, and I shrug. We need to add answering interview questions to things we practice. We didn't, so I'm going to have to wing this and hope I don't say something asinine.

"If I'm doing something, I'm going to give it my all," I say. "Whether it's hockey or dancing or law school, whatever it is, I'm all in and wanna be the best."

DeeDee gasps. "You're a lawyer too?"

I nod. I know this info was part of the media package the show provided and not a secret, but I play along.

"How are you still single?" She nudges Sophie with her elbow and winks. "Unless he's not?"

I ignore the innuendo. "Playing professional hockey was a dream of mine that I didn't think I'd ever get a chance to realize. I know this is Sophie's dream, and I want her to have what she's always wanted. A couple months of hard work is worth it to make her dreams come true too."

Truth is, I'm exhausted, and my body is taking a beating. But the brilliant smile and quick hug she gives me makes it worth it.

10

SOPHIE

I did it. Okay, we did it. I know it's a team effort, but *I did it*. I choreographed a dance the judges liked. I taught it to Trevor. He performed it well enough for us to get one of the top scores. The television audience enjoyed it enough to vote for us to stay, and I took my first step to being chosen as a pro dancer for the next season. It's going to happen.

The lights of the city cast shadows through the windows of the SUV limousine taking Trevor and me back to Atlantic City. Our friends and family that showed up for the first week's show drove the limo up. We didn't want to be rude and fly while they rode back, so we joined them.

"Champagne?" Bedard asks, holding up a bottle.

"Sure, thank you," I say. We're all shifters, and a glass of champagne won't make anyone tipsy. Well, Miranda isn't a shifter, but she's Irish, so the same holds true for her, too.

My phone vibrates in my coat pocket, so I pull it out. It's an email from the show's producers with next week's dance and song selection. We have the rumba. Rumba is a challenge at any time, but in week two, after the fast-paced, exuberant cha-cha? Being slow and sensual will be a big shift in gears. It's a very intimate dance. I'll listen to the track when I'm back in my room, but if it's the version I think it is, we're going to melt the dance floor next week.

"Everything okay?" Trevor asks. He's next to me on the bench seat of the limo, his body heat seeping into me. It's comforting. I'm exhausted after the long day and wish I could snuggle into his warmth and nap on the way home. I miss sleeping in his arms. While we were traveling for the road games, we slept apart because it would've been awkward being so obvious in front of the entire team and my brother. And when we were back in Atlantic City, we were caught up in extra dance practices, and Trevor had extra hockey practice and multiple home games. Even with willing spirits, having the time, place, and energy to be intimate beyond some quick kisses has been impossible. Hopefully after tonight, that will all change.

I nod. Even though the city lights are no longer streaming in, I know his night vision must be strong enough to see me. "Aye, they sent out what next week's dance is. Rumba."

His straight, white teeth flash with his smile. "You're tired. You said 'aye.' You sound especially Irish when you're tired or angry."

"I am tired," I admit. "Aren't you?"

Trevor shakes his head. "Not yet. I'm still riding the adrenaline high. It's the same way after a good game. I'll zonk out when we get home."

My intention is to stay awake with the others for the ride home. The reality is I fall asleep and am woken by Trevor gently jostling me and murmuring my name.

"Hmm..." I snuggle deeper under the covers. It's so warm and cozy. I sit up abruptly when I remember I'm not in bed and realize I spent the ride nestled against Trevor's side with his arm draped around me. I dislodge his arm, but I immediately miss the warmth and comfort.

Miranda's smirking at me. She wipes at her chin. Random, but okay. She widens her eyes and rubs at her chin quite deliberately. Slowly, I reach up and rub at mine and am horrified to find it's wet.

Crap, I drooled in my sleep. I surreptitiously look at Declan, but other than a single raised eyebrow, he's not reacting. That's good. There's nothing to react to. I've had a long day and long car rides lull me to sleep. It's been that way since I was a kid. What I did was perfectly natural. So was Trevor putting his arm around me to keep me steady. That's all it was.

I look out the vehicle window and am surprised not to see neon. We aren't at Devil's Den, we're at Trevor's home. It's dark now so I can't see anything but I know from being here New Year's Day that in addition to the barn Trevor renovated into apartments for him and his teammates to live in, there's the house Trevor grew up in with his siblings. That's where Mallory and Liam live. It's surrounded by woods full of trails to run on. His eldest brother has a cottage some-where on the expansive property and there are assorted outbuildings like a pool house and garages. Relatives own neighboring properties so it's almost like a big Carter family compound.

"I'll drive you back to Devil's Den," Trevor says. "It was easier to come here first to drop everyone else off."

"Or you can just stay over," Miranda says. Declan whips his head toward her.

She shrugs. "She can stay in your room. You don't sleep in there anymore." Her eyes widen like they would when we were little girls and she heard there were new kittens in the barn. "You could move here and take over Dec's room! It would cut down on the time wasted driving back and forth. You can practice here. Cutting out drive time would probably add another hour or two you guys could practice each day."

I know she's being logical and practical, but I do not want to live next door to my brother and my best friend. No matter how quiet they are, I'm going to hear things I don't want to. Would Trevor even want me around that much?

Kendall and Burke are the first out of the limo, and I follow. No matter what I end up doing, there's no reason to keep the limo here.

Before I can say anything, Mallory saves the day.

"Randi, you've only lived with Trevor for a few weeks, and you're all wrapped up in love with Mac. As someone who has lived with my brother for years and who loves him, your suggestion sucks. Trev and Sophie work together for hours every day. They'll be traveling together. For everyone's sake, they need their own space."

Trevor nods, and I try not to be offended. Because I don't want to be with him constantly. Hell, there are times I don't even want to be with *me*, let alone another person. Another reason to not get married. If I can't do a couple of months with someone, how can I do forever?

"However," Mallory turns to me. "Randi makes sense. Cutting down on drive time would give you more time to practice. If you don't want to move in here"—she waves a hand at the barn— "you're welcome to stay in the main house or the pool house. I think you'd like the pool house. It's a short walk through the stand of trees. Bedroom, bath, kitchen, laundry. Not as fancy as Devil's Den, of course."

A gust of icy wind makes me shiver.

"Let's discuss this tomorrow," Trevor says. "We're all too tired, and it's too cold to be standing out here making decisions. Sophie, if you're okay crashing here for tonight, that would be great, but no pressure. I'll drive you back to AC if you'd be more comfortable."

Liam and Mallory say goodnight and walk toward their home. Kendall and Burke are already upstairs.

"If you're sure you don't mind me staying over tonight," I say, "that sounds good. I'm exhausted and want to get some more sleep. We can discuss things tomorrow?" I look from my brother and Miranda to Trevor. They nod, and Miranda smiles.

"Ooh, I hope you move in, even to the pool house." She bounces on her toes and claps like she'd do on the sidelines as a cheerleader. I've watched videos of her and Trevor cheering to see what kind of things Trevor can do and get some inspiration for moves I can adapt. "We could hang out more, have girls' nights." Miranda leans forward and whispers, "Get away from the guys."

Declan and Trevor look away, their lips twitching. Miranda doesn't realize no matter how low she whispers, wolf shifters standing within three feet are going to hear her.

"I'll think about it," I whisper back. At my normal volume, I say, "Can we go upstairs? It's cold out here."

"Yeah, sorry," Trevor says. "Let's go."

I follow him up the stairs to the apartment, admiring the way his jeans hug his arse. Hockey apparently sculpts muscle into divine proportions. The warmth of the apartment is welcome after the frigid chill outside.

"Do you want cocoa or warmed milk?" Declan asks as we take off our coats. His question makes me smile. That's what Ma would make for us as kids before bed. I suspect there may have been a wee bit of whisky in there on days we were particularly ornery. That's what I'd do. Another reason it's a good thing I'm not planning on being a mother.

"No, I'm okay. I won't have any problems falling asleep. Just point me in the direction of a bed." Glancing at Miranda, I ask, "Do you have something I can borrow to sleep in?"

"Of course. Let's get you settled." She leads the way down the hallway. "Everything is fresh," she says over her shoulder.

This room is a twin to Miranda's room, but in a more masculine style. The furniture is dark wood, and the bedding is navy blue. Smiling, I spontaneously hug Miranda. I think it surprises her as much as it surprises me. I'm not usually a hugger, but that's something I'd like to change. Especially with Miranda. For so long, we haven't been close. Part of that was interference from Doreen and her cursed tea, but my own jealousy was to blame, too. I don't have any close girl-friends. In the dance world, we're always competing against each other, and just like my romantic relationships, women would pretend to be my friends to get closer to my family and advance their careers. Miranda has been my only loyal friend, even during the time we were apart. I know she'll marry Declan one day and we'll be sisters as well as best friends.

I'm envious that she has a group of girlfriends here already. I wish I had that. Maybe once I'm a permanent pro on the show, I can be friends with the other dancers. If I'm not going to have a man and a family in my future, then I want to have a group of friends. I don't want to be alone.

"Here you go," Miranda says, handing me a T-shirt and sleep pants. "I put a new toothbrush and deodorant on the counter. You're welcome to my shampoo or anything else you need."

"Thanks," I say.

As she's about to go through the bathroom that connects this bedroom with hers, she turns to add, "The guys have practice at ten in the morning. My schedule is flexible. If you want to go later than that, it's not a problem." She comes back into the room and bends to give me a hug. "I know you're only here for a little while because of the show, but I'm so excited we're going to be able to spend more time together. This is a dream come true for me. The man I love, my best friends, a home—these are things I was afraid to wish for when I was younger because I knew I'd never have them. Half the time, I expect to wake up and discover this was all a dream. But this really is my life now. It can be your life too."

I think about what Miranda said as I prepare for bed. Her dreams are coming true. Mine are too. It's a shame they're taking us in different directions.

11

TREVOR

BREAKFAST IS A FREE-FOR-ALL. A FEW TIMES A WEEK, WE'LL DO SOMETHING as a group, usually if we can get Stone to cook. He's the best cook of all of us, and he enjoys it the most, but today, we're on our own. I'm waiting for Sophie to join us before I make any decisions, in case she'd rather go somewhere for breakfast. I want to be hospitable.

Randi's seated at the counter when Sophie exits the bedroom.

"Good morning!" Randi says cheerfully when she sees her. "Would you like some cocoa?"

Sophie nods. "Still off drinking tea? I haven't had any since we discovered what Doreen was doing."

"Aye. Of all the things I'm angry at her for, ruining tea for me is the most heinous."

"It's okay. Do you have yogurt? Where's the cocoa?"

I join her at the counter and gently nudge her out of the way to open a drawer. I hand her a spoon before turning to open the refrigerator and reaching back to hand Sophie a container of yogurt. "Do you want berries?" I ask with my head still inside the fridge. When she doesn't answer, I turn and find her gaze fixed on my ass. I'm wearing team-branded sweatpants. Nothing sexy. They aren't even gray like the ladies go crazy for, they're basic black. But if she enjoys the view, I'm not going to complain.

"Berries would be nice, thank you." Her voice is husky.

Randi snorts from her seat behind us, and I turn around in time to catch her smirk. I hand Sophie the container of mixed berries and reach into the drawer for a spoon of my own. I take back the container of mixed berries and dump some into my own cup of yogurt. I hold it up to do a toast and am met with a blank expression. I huff out an exasperated breath and roll my eyes before tapping my yogurt container against Sophie's with a murmured "cheers."

"Soph, we're supposed to be partners. Understand what the other is going to do and follow along," I grumble.

Now Mac and Randi are chuckling. The red flush climbing up Sophie's neck doesn't bode well for me.

She quirks an eyebrow that seems to convey *let's make everyone uncomfortable.* Slowly slipping the spoon from between her lips, she establishes eye contact with me. Licking a drop of yogurt off the tip of the spoon elicits a gulp from me and a slight warning growl from Mac. Her mischievous grin tells me she's having fun and that this is partly revenge for seeing way too much of Mac and Randi being lovey-dovey. Turnabout is fair play.

"Well, Trev, we are partners. On the dance floor." She gives a saucy wink. "So far."

Mac growls again, making Sophie grin. I'm kinda scared, though. I hope he doesn't put cooling gel in my protective cup. I'm not going to leave it unguarded in the locker room. "Forgive me for not real-izing yogurt toasts are a thing here. I'll try to do better next time." With a sexily arched brow, she spoons up more yogurt and closes her eyes with an orgasmic groan as she swallows.

My dick starts to harden. I can't help but imagine what it would feel like if she swallowed with my cock deep in her mouth. Now I feel a flush creeping up my neck, too. The tips of my ears are probably as red as the goal lamp.

"Anyway," Mac says, apparently deciding it's best to ignore our shenanigans rather than continuing to growl. "You think you want to live in the pool house, Soph?"

"Mhm mm uh," she says. I assume she's saying, "I don't know."

She goes to pick up her mug and realizes she never made her cocoa. Wordlessly, I reach into the black-and-white lighthouse cookie jar on the counter and pull out a packet.

"Thanks," she says, shaking the packet before ripping it open and dumping it in the mug of hot water Randi poured her. Using the spoon from her yogurt, she stirs in the powder. I take her empty yogurt container and rinse it along with mine, then put them in the recycling bin under the sink and throw her cocoa packet in the trash. I like to have things tidy.

"Pool house?" Mac asks.

"Oh, yeah. No reason not to look at it. With how much we're traveling, I don't need anything incredible. The room at Devil's Den is gorgeous, but I feel bad tying it up for so long."

She rolls her shoulders. I can see the tension she's carrying. I'd be happy to rub her shoulders—or other parts—to help ease it.

"And I'd rather be near the woods. I can't shift and run there with all that sand and the city."

"It's nice," I say. "I think you'll like it. And if you don't, not a big deal. I'm fine driving back and forth for practice. Don't change things to make it easier for me. Do what's best for you."

That seems to bring her up short. I don't know what I said that was wrong. I'm trying to be nice.

"Okay." She tilts her head toward the bedroom she stayed in. "Can we talk for a sec?"

Randi and Mac share a glance, silently communicating something I probably don't want to know.

"Yeah, of course," I say before following her down the hall into the bedroom. I close the door behind me for privacy, knowing it's pointless. Mac can hear what we say if he wants.

She turns to face me, her hands clasped together. I think she's trying to disguise that they're shaking. What reason would she have to be nervous around me?

"Are you sure it's okay if I move to the pool house?" she asks and then licks her lips. Another sign of nervousness. I don't get it. "We're together so much already with practice and traveling. I don't want to crowd you and make your home uncomfortable. We're wolf shifters. We can be territorial even though we like to have a pack around us. I'm not part of your pack."

My wolf wholeheartedly disagrees with that sentiment. If I was to have a pack, Sophie would be at the center of it. I reach out and pull one of her hands free from the tight clasp they're locked in. Lacing my fingers with hers, I tug gently to pull her closer. She could stand her ground, but she moves easily into my embrace. Wrapping my free arm around her waist and resting our clasped hands against my chest, I look down into her beautiful blue eyes. They're the clear blue of the summer sky, not the murky blue of the Atlantic Ocean in winter.

"I want you to do what makes you happy and what you're comfortable with." On impulse, I drop a kiss on her forehead. I wish I could've placed it about four inches lower, but I know once we start it's hard to stop, and these joggers won't hide my reaction. "I know Randi loves the idea of you being closer so you can spend more time together. Mac too. As far as I'm concerned, you're welcome to this room, but I understand how that may be too close for comfort for everyone."

I fist her shirt where my hand rests on her hip. My gaze drops to her mouth. My wolf instincts have me licking my lips, wanting to pounce. Only my steely control keeps me from eating her up.

"To be honest, this fling we're supposedly having with each other might actually happen if we're closer."

Her eyes ignite with desire, and her hands fist in my shirt then open flat to press against my chest. Feeling my muscles seems to cause her breath to catch, to race.

"Yes," she says, her gaze lingering on my mouth, her hips pressing against mine in clear invitation.

"What are we going to tell everyone? I don't want to keep this a secret from your brother and our friends. I don't want to sneak around."

"Is there a reason we wouldn't keep it a secret?" she asks. "We'd be having fun, but it wouldn't be anything serious. If our friends and my brother know, then there'll be questions when it's over. I'm not going to be here, so you're going to be the one stuck dealing with the fallout. Is that something you want to deal with?"

I shrug. "I don't care who knows. Everyone at least suspects something is going on because of the nights I've spent at the hotel. You stayed in my room at the All-Star Game. Who knows who saw us kissing on New Year's or in the bar in Florida."

"Yeah, but I stayed in your room at the All-Star Game because of Miranda and Declan."

I laugh. "I know what you said, but that doesn't mean anyone believed it."

She flicks her hand nonchalantly. "Whatever. I don't care. Tell whoever you want whatever you want, then. But I don't want to discuss it on the show. People will suspect a showmance because they always do, but it's a double-edged sword. If we make it public, folks who ship us will vote for you, but we risk alienating the people who vote for you because they think you're unattached. If we keep it vague, then everyone believes what they want and you'll get your votes. Win-win!"

I loosen my grip, allowing her to step out of my embrace to go back to the kitchen where Dec and Miranda are clearing their breakfast dishes.

"Ready to go see Mallory?" Randi asks. When Sophie says she is, they put on their coats and follow me and Mac outside to wave goodbye as we drive away in Dec's SUV.

Mac drums his fingers on his steering wheel in a rhythm only he can hear. Am I making both of the Mackenzie siblings nervous today?

"What's going on with you and Sophie?" he asks abruptly, his Scottish brogue deeper than usual.

Mac's my friend, and I'm not going to insult him by pretending to not understand what he's asking. "We've kissed a few times, and I'm attracted to her, but nothing beyond that. Yet. I won't lie to you. Or to Sophie. I want your sister. But I'm not cut out to have a relationship. I'm not like you. I'm not looking for the white picket fence and kids. We're having a fling while we're doing the show and she's here. Provided we can get time alone together," I say pointedly, causing Mac to chuckle.

"Hey, I'm all for it. But don't hurt her. Be upfront about what you want. She's been used by men trying to get closer to our family." He raises his hand to cut off my protest. "I know you're not like that. But be careful with this fling. Make sure she doesn't start wishing for forever when you're looking for right now."

Now it's my turn to nervously drum my fingers against my thigh. Mac is one of my best friends. I don't want this to cause a problem between us.

The trees whiz by as I think.

"I'm monogamous, and I'm honest. I don't lead anyone on. The hookups I've had always knew that's all it was. Sophie knows. I never want to hurt her. I care about her. But I'm not cut out for marriage."

If I ever did get married, I'd want it to be to someone like Sophie. But I could never make her happy and give her what she wants.

And I'd rather my heart be broken than hers.

12

SOPHIE

I LOVE THE POOL HOUSE AND MAKE ARRANGEMENTS TO MOVE IN AS SOON AS possible. It's decorated exactly in my style, like it was meant for me.

"So, what's your plan for today?" Miranda asks as we walk through the trees back to the barn.

I chew my bottom lip. "Are you going to the rink today?"

She nods. "Do you want to come with me?"

"Yeah. I need to let Teagan know I'll be staying here and pack up my things. Trevor and I will practice this afternoon. It's the rumba this week."

Miranda grins and wiggles her eyebrows. "Ooh, sexy. Have you slept together yet?"

I stumble over air. Not a question I was expecting from Miranda. "Why do you ask?"

"Because I'm nosy," she answers frankly. "You guys have chemistry like crazy. I know how Trevor is with women. The signs are there."

"What do you mean by, how he is with women? How is he?" I know we're having a fling—that better be consummated tonight before I explode in a flaming pile of frustrated goo—but I don't want to be part of a cast of thousands.

"Um...well...he likes to play the field. He's not a jerk about it, but he's not a relationship type of guy. He treats them well, but it's always casual. I'm surprised he gets away with it, but he's charming."

"Aye..." He's certainly charming. And I fall for it every time. "That's fine. I'm not looking for a relationship. We haven't had sex yet because the night we were going to do the deed my best friend and brother cockblocked us, and since then, we've been surrounded by the team or exhausted from all our practices to do anything. We get to kiss some and make out in dark corners when we have a moment, but that's not satisfying. Anyway, it would be a fling, not forever. We'll be scratching some itches for the time we're together, nothing more than that." I stop and look up at the sky, my breath making puffy white clouds. "Miranda, I'm so...itchy. It's torture being near him and touching him all the time but not being able to *touch* him. It's driving me mad. When we're done with the show, we'll move on. He has hockey here, and I'll be preparing for the next season of the show in New York or wherever. But lordy, I need my itches scratched in the worst way—and soon. By him."

As we exit the band of trees and approach the barn, Miranda says, "Long-distance relationships are a thing, you know."

I sigh. "Yes, they are. I don't want one."

I take a few more steps before I realize that Miranda stopped walking. Glancing over my shoulder, I try to determine why she stopped.

"You could commute. New York isn't that far. Buses go to and from the casinos every day." She has an excited gleam in her eyes.

Oh no. I need to quash this idea right now so she doesn't get her hopes up. So I don't start thinking about things I have no business thinking about. "You know all this time I spend with Trevor? I need to do that with every partner. This isn't a job I can work remotely. For months each year, I'd be with that partner. And Trevor would travel for hockey. We'd never be together. That's no way to have a relationship."

"It's a few months each year, and it overlaps, so you'd both be busy. Then you'd have free time to be together. It could work."

"Okay. But I don't want to make it work. I don't want a relationship beyond now. So let's drop this and focus on you and I enjoying being together again." I loop my arm through hers and continue next to her, back to the barn.

When we arrive in Atlantic City, I go up to my room in Devil's Den while Miranda goes to her office in The Nest. It doesn't take me long to pack my belongings. What takes the most time is gathering my courage to call Teagan and tell her I'm moving out. I appreciate her generosity in letting me stay in this gorgeous suite. I'm hoping I don't offend her or make her think I'm ungrateful.

Okay, Sophie, be a brave wolf. It's just a phone call. Not a big deal. Taking a deep breath, I pick up my cell phone and dial Teagan's phone number. A few minutes later I'm shaking my head over how silly I was to worry.

Calling down to the front desk, I arrange for them to keep my bags there so they can do what they need to get the suite ready for future use, then I head to the theater to work on the choreography for this week's rumba. It's a sexy dance all about sensual movement, precise footwork, and connection. It's going to be a challenge to make it seem like we're connected sexually when we're not. I know the show likes to promote showmances and the fans like to speculate, but I don't want my real life to be fodder for gossip. Especially when the relationship will only last as long as we're on the show.

Nigel and Nancy show up and suggest we go over to the rink to get some footage of Trevor at practice. I protest because we haven't cleared that with the team, but Nancy insists. I shoot Miranda a text so she can stop us at the door if necessary. No such luck. She thinks it's a great idea and meets us to act as our escort to the practice rink. The team looks like it's broken into four squads based on the four colors of jerseys they're wearing—black, white, blue, and gray.

Trevor's in a blue jersey. I have no idea what the specific drill is, but Trevor shoots the puck to a skater on his right and then speeds toward the goal. The other skater passes it to a teammate across the ice, who then fires it to Trevor. Somehow the puck bounces off Trev's stick and into the goal. They run a different version of the drill that has Trevor doing the passing and his teammate somehow redirecting the puck into the goal. Other squads run the same drill, but it looked best when Trevor did it.

"Hey," he says when he skates over. He's removed his helmet, and his copper-toned hair is darkened with sweat.

"Hi," I say, feeling shy. "I wanted to see you on the ice. What was the drill you were doing?"

He looks over his shoulder toward the ice like he needs to jog his memory.

"Deflection drill. Practicing getting into position so we can take advantage of pucks

sneaking through and target them into the goal without actively shooting. Sometimes hockey is about lucky breaks just as much as it's about pure skill."

Chuckling, I nod. "So is dance."

His smile is so warm, I'm surprised the ice isn't melting.

I make a show of taking a big sniff and scrunching my nose. "Go shower and meet me for practice. Maybe we'll get lucky with the rumba." My cheeks flame when I realize my choice of phrase. "See you in the theater."

Half an hour later, Trevor comes striding in the studio backstage of the theater. He must have rushed through the shower and raced across the Boardwalk into the hotel because his hair is still damp, but now it's clean and he doesn't smell all sweaty. Sometimes he smells good when he's sweaty, but that's after we've danced. Dance sweat is different from sport sweat. We do our banter bit and then jump right into learning the basic movements of the dance.

"The rumba is all about the connection between us," I say for the camera's sake. "It's a sensual dance. Lots of rhythmic, fluid motion and hip action. We shift our weight to create figure-eight motions with our hips." I demonstrate, then motion for Trevor to follow along. He kind of gets it, but he's not getting the swivel needed. "You're doing more hula hoop and less rumba. Here." I place my hands on his hips and help guide him through the motion. Heat flares in his hazel eyes, and I wonder if he's imagining us doing some naked rumba practice tonight in my new bedroom.

"Okay," he says when he has the basics of the hip motion down. "What do I do with my arms?"

"You want to make sure you take up lots of space when you dance. Your arms will have their own fluid motions, and you want to make sure you complete the movements. Don't cut them short. You can't dance small. That's something they dinged us on yesterday. I can match you, so you don't need to dance down to me. I'll follow you."

The lecherous grin that spreads across Trevor's lips will not get edited out. Damn it.

We spend the next two hours working on the beginning counts of the dance. Even though this is my job, the way we have to touch and move suggestively really turns me on. If the bulge in his track pants is anything to go by, it's affecting Trevor, too.

"Are you packed?" he asks after Nancy and Nigel leave.

I smile. "Aye. Tonight I'll be staying in the pool house."

Pulling me close, he presses a kiss to my lips.

"What was that for?" I ask when we break apart after a few intense moments of kissing and above-the-belt caresses.

His eyebrows almost reach his hairline. "I couldn't resist. Do you mind?"

Smirking, I rest my hand on his chest. The steady beat of his heart tempts me to create a dance to match it. "Does it feel like I minded?"

"No, but it doesn't hurt to double-check. Having you next door is going to be very convenient."

We grab my luggage from the front desk and get in his car to drive home. Turning on the highway that takes us off the island and toward home, he changes the subject. "Did you want to stop to get some groceries?"

I hadn't thought about having a kitchen and needing to feed myself. I can cook, but I rarely have the opportunity to. Or the motivation. Since I have a shifter metabolism and burn a lot of calories dancing anyway, I can get away with takeaway curries or whatever else I want delivered to my flat in London. Out in the woods, there aren't as many options.

"That would be grand, thank you."

American grocery stores are fascinating places. They're huge. Everything is so big: the store, the packaging, the variety of things. An entire long aisle is just breakfast cereal. So many varieties and so many sizes of the same thing. It's crazy. I push the trolley, and Trevor grabs what I want. It's an efficient system since I wouldn't be able to reach half the things because the shelves are so high. That's an advantage of having a tall boyfriend.

No. Oh no. I stop dead as Trevor walks on. I don't know where that thought came from, but Trevor is *not* my boyfriend. Boyfriends don't have expiration dates.

"Are you okay?" he asks when he walks back to me. Concern shines in his eyes in a touch of gray clouds I hate to see.

"Aye, just amazed at all of this. It's different from London."

He looks around. "Oh. I've never been to London. Do you miss it? Maybe we could visit."

The deer-in-the-headlights expression on his face tells me he didn't mean to suggest making plans for the future any more than I meant to mentally call him my boyfriend. Our brains go on autopilot sometimes. That doesn't mean it's what our hearts want.

"Uh...I mean, maybe I'll get there someday. Not that we would go together. I know that's not happening." He blushes adorably. A pang hits me in my chest. It's affection for this man, but also sadness I won't get to show him around London. Show him all the places I love.

Nodding, I give what I hope passes for a smile. "Let me know if you want any suggestions on things to see, restaurants, where not to go."

We continue up and down the aisles, and he adds things to the trolley that he likes. I don't think he realizes the assumption he's making that he's going to be in my place enough to eat all of it. Not that I say anything to disabuse him of the notion he'll be there at breakfast to drink the extra pulpy orange juice I can't stand. I just follow him and point out the things I like as we discuss the team's travel plans to figure out when we'll be cooking dinner. Together. Like a couple. But we're not a couple. I heard about how Kendall and Burke started out fake dating and fell in love, but that's not what this is, and we aren't them.

The pasta we make for dinner is delicious, and Trevor is good company as we wash the dishes as a team. Holding his hand as I lead him upstairs, I think about how much I enjoyed cooking dinner together. Other men I was involved with didn't set foot into the kitchen, and most of our time was spent in the studio or in the bedroom. If we had dinner, it was at a fancy restaurant when they were trying to seduce me or something I threw together when I was trying to keep them.

Entering the bedroom, his eyes roam the space. His smile is wistful when he says, "This room suits you."

I unpack my first suitcase while he sits on the chair. He offers to help, but there isn't really anything he can do other than keep me company.

"Funny you should say that." I put a pile of leggings in the dresser drawer.

"Oh?"

"This is the furniture and bedding I have back at home."

He looks around and seems to pay more attention to every detail, like it'll tell secrets about me or something.

"Really? Exactly?"

"I noticed it when I toured the place earlier today. It's one of the reasons I decided to stay here."

I unlock my phone and swipe to the picture of me taking a selfie in a sundress. You can see the bed and nightstands in the background.

His finger hovers like he wants to swipe to look at more of my pictures, but good manners and self-preservation stop him from following through. Not that I have anything to hide in the photos on my phone, but it's rude to snoop. His parents may have been less than ideal in the attention department, but they taught him manners.

"That confirms you belong here." He stands, crosses the room, puts my phone on the dresser, and then takes me in his arms to kiss me with a mixture of sweetness and thoroughness that makes my tummy flip and my toes scrunch against the bedroom rug. His hands gently frame my face as his kiss moves from my lips to my jaw, down my neck, and to my shoulder. Little nips and quick licks accompany the kisses. Goosebumps break out across my skin. He clasps my hands and interlaces our fingers.

Our dance lessons are paying off. He uses his body to direct me to the closet door as if he's leading in a dance. With my back against the door, he steps closer, one of his thighs slipping between my leggings-covered ones as his torso brushes against mine. Trevor raises our joined hands above my head and uses one of his to hold them there. I know I'm not trapped. If I said no or struggled at all, he'd step away. But I'm enjoying this show of dominance. We're going to set the ballroom on fire with our passion.

I rub my center against his thigh, desperate for the friction I need. Trevor's erection is solid and hard against my abdomen. We're burning for each other.

"Please," I moan.

"Please what?" he whispers. "Please more? Please stop? Please take my clothes off? You're going to have to be more specific with your requests, princess."

This time when he calls me princess, it doesn't feel like snark. It's said with affection, and it touches something within me. Not that spot where I want the something currently stiff against my abdomen hitting, though.

"Please naked. Please bed. Please now."

"As you wish."

I don't know if he knows he's making a *Princess Bride* reference or not, but it makes me smile nonetheless. He releases his grip on my wrist so I can help with our disrobing. We get a bit tangled trying to remove each other's shirts, pants, and underwear. It's obvious I didn't choreograph this. I'm not sure what to expect when I see his cock for the first time. He's been blessed with length and girth, but not ridiculously so. I've never slept with another wolf shifter—or any shifter—before. My previous partners have been human. I think the fact I was a shifter caused them to have sexual expectations of me I didn't live up to. Like that I prefer doggy style. I don't. Back when I was hoping to feel connected to my partners, I wanted missionary. I wanted to be facing each other.

I wonder what Trevor expects. When we're naked and stretched out on the bed, I expect our joining to be frantic and explosive. However, it's slow and tender. Brushes of fingertips, lingering kisses, sighs, and murmurs of "yes" and "ooh, I like that." As good as every-thing feels, I can't stop the worrying thoughts pushing into my mind. What if I don't satisfy him? What if I don't know how to do something that's expected of me as a wolf shifter?

I must tense up because suddenly he stops nuzzling my neck and is rolling off me to hold himself up with a forearm.

"What's wrong? Did you change your mind? It's okay if you did, we'll stop. If you don't like something, Sophie, just tell me." His eyes are hazy with lust, but I can see the concern in his expression. He would stop. That's how every man should react, but I know that's not always the case. It makes me want him even more. And makes me more afraid of disappointing him.

"Hey, talk to me." He runs his calloused fingertips gently along my jaw.

"I...I haven't done this before," I whisper. When his eyes widen, I realize how that sounds. "I mean, I've done *this* before. I'm not a virgin. But I haven't slept with another shifter. Is there something different about it? Doggy style?" I'm blushing, and if it was possible to pull the covers over my head and hide in embarrassment, I would.

His brows pull down in consternation. "Do you like doggy style? I want to give you what you want, but that's not my go-to. It feels so impersonal, and that's not what I want with you."

His chest expands with a deep breath and slow release.

"Should we be getting dressed and talking? We don't need to rush into anything. Your pleasure and comfort are what matter to me. If you're uncomfortable going any further, we can get dressed and watch a movie. I can go back to the barn." He gestures to his cock. "I obviously want you." As if to emphasize the point, a drop of precum drips onto my thigh. "But I want you to want this too. I care about you, Sophie."

My last shield crumbles. My heart is going to be broken when this is over, and I may break his heart, too. But it's going to be worth it.

Resting my hand on the back of his neck, I pull him down into a kiss. I pour all my yearning and desire into it. I want this man. His body, his pleasure, and lord help me, his heart. But for tonight, I'll settle for the first two.

"I want this, Trevor. I want you," I say between kisses. "I want to hold you and see you as we do this." I pull back from our kisses so I can look into his eyes. "Is that okay?"

He nuzzles my cheek with his nose. There's a tug low in my core. I want this man. I hope he still wants me, too.

Trevor presses the gentlest, sweetest kiss to the corner of my mouth and rubs his chin along my jaw. His scruff is ticklish, and I better not have beard burn in the morning.

"More than okay," he murmurs, kissing his way down my neck

and to my breasts. He's now resting with his weight upon me, but I don't feel suffocated. I feel cozy. He's so tall, his torso is over my lower abdomen and between my legs. His large hands completely engulf my breasts as he caresses one while kissing and sucking on the other. I'm not overly endowed, a B cup, but they're firm and perky and, if his moans and low growls of pleasure are any indication, completely enough to please Trevor. The attention he's paying to my breasts, while appreciated, makes me want him inside me. Now. I know I should be doing more in the foreplay department than lying back and enjoying his attention, but he's getting so much pleasure from giving it, it feels rude not to relish in receiving. I'll take care of him next time.

"Trevor," I whisper.

"Hmm?" he hums as he licks his way to my navel, lifting his lust-filled eyes to mine.

"Do you have a condom?" Please let him have a condom. I'm on the pill, and I know my cycle, so I shouldn't be fertile, but I don't want to risk anything. Shifters rarely get STIs, and I know hockey players are tested by team doctors regularly, so I'm not overly concerned about that, but I always use a condom. No glove, no love, as they say.

"Yeah," he says, licking around my belly button before pressing a kiss to it and then blowing a raspberry. I giggle, and he looks up with a boyish grin. "Should I be getting it?"

I nod. In a flash, he's retrieved a couple of foil squares from his wallet and is stretching to put one on the nightstand.

"For round two," he says, waggling his eyebrows.

I mentally add a box of condoms to my grocery list.

Sitting up, I hold out my hand. "Let me."

I roll the condom he produced from his wallet onto his hard cock. Once sheathed by the latex, he gives his shaft a couple of strokes as he kisses me, easing me back against the duvet. The cotton is cool on my skin, but it feels nice in contrast to the heat radiating from Trevor's body. His weight settles on top of me, and the head of his cock brushes through my folds. I know I cheated myself on foreplay, but I'm dying to have him inside me, filling me in a way I'm sure no other man has been able to. We can do more foreplay next time. This time I want to get to the main event.

We're kissing as he eases his length into me, stretching me, filling me. We both sigh with pleasure when he's fully seated. I clench my inner muscles, and he growls. I've never made a man growl before. I don't know if it's a shifter thing or a Trevor thing. All I know is that I love it.

"Sophie, love," Trevor says, between nibbles, kissing to a spot below my right ear that I didn't know was connected to my clit. "If you keep doing that, this isn't going to last very long."

Love. I know it's just a casual term of endearment and doesn't mean anything, but I wish it did. I know I'm going to regret all of this when it's over and I'm a brokenhearted mess. But I don't care. It's worth it to feel what I'm feeling now.

He starts a steady rhythm of deep thrusts and even works in some of the rumba hip swivels I taught him earlier. I think naked rumba moves are my new favorite. He thrusts faster and harder, and tension coils inside me. We're still kissing, and my hands are roaming over his strong shoulders and down his muscled back. His hands have been tracing my curves and gripping my hips. When he slips one between us to massage my clit, I tumble over the edge into the most earth-shattering orgasm of my life. I call out Trevor's name, and with another two thrusts and a satisfied moan, Trevor falls over the cliff with me. As we lay tangled together, sweaty and catching our breaths, I realize we aren't having sex. We're making love. And I'm terrified.

13
TREVOR

I POSITION SOPHIE IN FRONT OF ME AS WE GET THE JUDGES' COMMENTS ON our rumba. I'm semihard, and the dance belt is helping hold my dick down, but it's a scrap of fabric, not a miracle worker. Sophie feels the burgeoning boner against her back and looks up at me with panic in her blue eyes. We decided we're not going public with our relationship. Let the audience and media assume what they want, but we're not confirming anything.

"That hip action!" Carlo is standing and swiveling his hips. "Superb!" He accents that with a chef's kiss gesture.

Glen nods. "I can tell you two put in a lot of hard work this week. It was a very sensuous rumba without being vulgar. Good job."

Sophie is wheezing, trying not to laugh at the phrase "hard work." I perfected the figure-eight hip action most nights this week in bed with Sophie. Miranda and my teammates have figured out we're sleeping together, but everyone's being cool about it. Ian's giving me a narrowed-eye glare. We didn't tell him about our fling, but it appears we didn't have to. I pray he doesn't say anything.

"Wow!" Mary Ann says, flopping back in her chair like she's boneless and spent. "I think we all need a cigarette after that one!

Not that you should smoke. Smoking is bad. But...yeah. That was smoking hot. Like Glen says, it was sensuous without being vulgar, and boy, was it sexy!"

Our scores keep us toward the top of the leaderboard, and the audience votes keep us in the competition.

"Hey, twinkle toes." Fessel, the coyote shifter from the Omaha Ogres, faces me at center ice with a nasty gleam in his eyes as we wait for the puck to drop. "Think I'm going to dance next year so I can fuck that hot piece of ass too." No doubt every single shifter on the ice heard what he said. Bedard and Mac give low warning growls— directed at me. They don't want me to lose my shit. And to this asshole too. Fighting is expressly forbidden in the PHL because we don't want people thinking shifters are violent. If we fight, it's not just two minutes in the penalty box. Punishment includes multiple game suspensions, hefty fines, and the possibility of having your contract canceled. You could even be kicked out of the league. I can't risk my position on the team. But it's tempting.

The puck drops, and I fire it back to Bedard, who skates through the neutral zone on a direct line to Fessel. Mac is headed that way too. Oh, no. Bedard shoots the puck directly toward Fessel, and the idiot doesn't have enough sense to let it go by. He gets the puck on the blade of his stick, grinning like he did something incredible. I grimace at the crunch Fessel makes as he becomes the filling in a Bedard and Mac sandwich. I gotta give him credit, he only lets out a yip and stays on his feet when Mac takes the puck from him.

"Never talk about my sister again, prick, or you won't be skating for a long time," Mac says menacingly as he skates off and calmly shoots the puck into the Ogres' goal as if it's empty.

We're playing in Nebraska, so there's no cheering crowd to celebrate, but the boos that rain down only spur us on to make two more goals. We ultimately win the game three to one, breaking our three-game losing streak. I hate that it was someone talking shit about Sophie that lit the fire. I also hate that I wasn't the one to stand up for her. That should be my right. As her boyfriend.

That word—boyfriend—brings me up short as I change in the visitors' locker room after showering. I'm not her boyfriend. I'm her lover, her friend with benefits. *Boyfriend* is not a role I'm suited to play. I don't know why that popped into my head. I got slammed against the board a few times and will have new aches and bruises in the morning, but I didn't hit my head. I don't have a concussion.

Sophie's blue eyes are dark with concern when I climb in the back of the SUV taking us to the airport and gingerly sit next to her.

"Trevor! Oh my god, are you okay? You took a lot of hard hits tonight. It's like they were targeting you. Are they allowed to do that?"

"It's just part of the game, Sophie. I'm okay."

She takes my hand and laces our fingers together. "I know, but tonight just seemed more...vicious."

I shrug, then regret it as pain lances through my shoulder. "That's just how the game is sometimes. Not a big deal."

I'm trying to reassure Sophie so she doesn't worry, but the truth is the Ogres decided to target me in retribution for what Bedard and Mac did to Fessel. He didn't play in the second or third periods due to an undisclosed injury.

The chirps I'm getting are nastier and more plentiful with each week. If it's this bad after three weeks, how much worse is it going to get? I wouldn't care if they were just ragging on me, but the vile things some of them are saying about Sophie make me see red.

And the hits. No one's going to go after my teammates—they're huge—so I'm the next best target. I'm not small, but I'm smaller than either of them. I also have the puck a lot, which makes me fair game. I've never been targeted like I am now. As a hockey player, I'm used to getting banged up and playing through pain, but usually I have days off and time to rest and heal.

I don't have that now. We're dancing every day. It's not as

punishing as getting smashed into the boards by a 220-pound steamroller, but it's difficult. I'm using different muscles and doing the same thing over and over. It's mentally taxing too. Trying to remember the moves, focus on making sure I'm in the right spot so Sophie doesn't get hurt, not thinking about what I'm missing by not being on the ice for practice. I'm exhausted. I don't want to be benched from a game, even though my body would welcome the rest. The show is too important to Sophie for me to not give it my best shot at keeping us in. This isn't forever. I only need to be strong for a few more weeks. It'll get better. But dancing tomorrow night is going to be a bitch.

Sophie and I are flying commercial to New York tonight and sleeping the best we can in first class before spending the day in costume fittings, dress rehearsal, and the live show. The team is flying to Colorado tomorrow, and we'll meet them there courtesy of another red-eye flight after tomorrow night's show. I can't wait to sleep in a bed—my bed—again.

We've been staying in the pool house, but I need a nice long soak in my gigantic tub followed by at least eight solid hours of unconsciousness on my mattress. Sophie's bed is comfy, especially because she's in it with me, but my mattress at home is the exact firmness that supports and cradles me the best. I wonder if Sophie would be okay staying in my apartment with me or if she'd feel awkward with her brother and Miranda there too. Would Mac be cool with it? By the time we're back in New Jersey, I'm not sure I'll even have the energy to get a boner, let alone fool around with Sophie, so I don't see what he could take issue with.

It's the fourth week of live shows, and we've just performed our salsa. The Omaha Ogres spent all night smashing me into the boards last night, and my ribs ache, so I'm struggling to catch my breath. I have a slight groin strain and a tweaked shoulder to go with the bruised ribs. I hurt everywhere. I know in a day or two, I'll be all healed up thanks to my shifter metabolism, but it's going to suck until then. And I have a game tomorrow.

"Are you okay?" Sophie whispers. I nod. I didn't tell her about my ribs. She's learning about hockey but doesn't always recognize the hits for what they are, and I don't want to worry her. I can handle this.

"I'm fine," I say, squeezing her waist out of reflex. When she slips her arm around my waist and squeezes in return, I hiss out a breath.

"Are you hurt?" She goes to unbutton my shirt right there on camera while we're waiting for feedback from the judges.

I give the most convincing smile I'm capable of and grab her hands, giving them a gentle squeeze. "I'm fine, physical game last night. Not a big deal. Really." I turn her so her back is against my front and wrap my arms around her. The judges watch our exchange. Everyone has seen this. Crap. I'd sigh but taking that deep of a breath would hurt too much.

Mary Ann's brow creases with concern. "Are you okay, Trevor?"

"I'm fine."

Carlo gives his charming but lecherous grin. "You certainly are fine! That was one spicy salsa. Technically, it was wonderful, and there's an obvious connection between the two of you, but I'm concerned. You don't look like you're having fun anymore. You're doing everything right, but the spark of joy is gone."

I shrug. I can't answer. I'm not having fun. I'm stressed, I'm exhausted, I'm guilty that I'm letting down my team by having this show as a distraction. I can't give my team my all and give dancing with Sophie my all. I don't have that much. But the last thing I'm going to do is complain about it. A handful of weeks are all I have with Sophie and the show. That's assuming we make it to the finals. The way the Devil Birds have dropped in the standings because of our losses, the playoffs aren't guaranteed. My hockey season could be over soon too. I'll suck it up for a few more weeks and cherish every moment I have doing things people only dream of.

Hockey media loves to speculate if the show, and by extension, Sophie, is the reason my points production has dropped off and why the Devil Birds are losing more games. I know my teammates and management don't think that. Hockey is a team sport, and everyone says it's not all on my shoulders to make the goals and win the games. But it's hard not to internalize the chatter and let it screw with me. I'm doing everything possible to play the best I can while also dedicating every moment not taken up by hockey to learning new dances each week and performing them. And my best isn't good enough. We're losing hockey games, and our standings for the play-offs are dropping. We're falling each week on the leaderboard as dancers too. Our scores are holding steady, but that's not good enough when everyone is improving and raising their scores.

If this wasn't so important to Sophie's dreams, I'd be wishing for elimination so I'd only have to focus on hockey. But when the show is done, so is my time with Sophie, and I can't wish away time with her. We spend every night together, even if it's just sleeping in each other's arms. I've never had that before. If I spent the night in a woman's bed, it's because we fell asleep after sex, and I was gone by dawn.

Glen rests his elbows on the judges' desk and steeples his fingers. "At this stage, it's not enough that you get the steps correct. Performance is a major component of the scores. If two dancers are on the same level in terms of skill, performance is going to tip the scale in favor of one over the other. If you're still here next week, I hope you can find that spark again because you're too good of a dancer to lose because of this." He uses his index finger to point at his own face with a glum expression and rotates his wrist to draw a circular frame to emphasize his point.

Sophie gasps, and I want to, but it hurts. This is the first time our position in the competition feels in jeopardy. She tilts her head back and her worried eyes make my heart clench. I know how badly she wants this, and I feel like a loser, putting her dreams at risk because I'm overwhelmed. My instinct is to bend down and give her a reassuring kiss, but we've already revealed too much. Instead, I pull her flush against my body and give her another squeeze. She raises her hands and rests them on my forearms crossed over her torso, giving them a squeeze too. I think her touch is more about holding on tight out of anxiety though. I hate that.

We end up getting all eights, same as last week. But other teams are getting nines and even a ten. Staying the same isn't good enough. We aren't in the bottom two teams, so we avoid the stress of wondering if we're the team to go home. I'm grateful for that. More for Sophie than for me. This is all for her.

I'm so exhausted, I fall asleep before takeoff on the red-eye to Denver. Sophie's gentle nudge wakes me as we descend. We have a car waiting to drive us into Colorado Springs to meet the team. With the difference in time zones, it's around one in the morning. I think. To be honest, I'm not entirely certain what day it is.

"Are you okay?" Sophie gently squeezes my hand as we walk through the jetway into the airport. "I can get us a room in Denver for tonight. The driver too. And then we can drive down to meet the team in the morning."

I shake my head in answer to her question and to get my few working brain cells rubbing together again. "I'm fine. Don't worry. Let's just get to the team hotel and sleep for a while."

We get in the car and travel the hour or so south to Colorado Springs. I doze off, so we could've taken a side trip to Mars and I wouldn't have known it.

"Are you staying tonight?" Sophie asks as we get to her room. Her question is unexpected. Why wouldn't I stay with her? We've been together every night for weeks.

"That was my plan. Is that okay?"

She unlocks the door, and I follow her in.

"Of course it's okay." After I close the door behind me and lock it, she wraps her arms around my waist, gently, and rests her head on my chest. "I'm worried about you. If you need to sleep alone to get better rest or to be more comfortable, I want you to do that."

I run the back of my fingers down her cheek before embracing her. "I want to be here with you, Sophie. Nowhere else."

Tears shine in her eyes but don't fall. I'm grateful for that. She steps out of our embrace and takes my hand, turning toward the bed. We don't have sex in deference to my ribs and exhaustion. But even without intercourse, lying together with Sophie's hair splayed across my chest and her fingertips resting over my heart feels like the greatest intimacy I could have with a woman.

14

TREVOR

"No practice for you today, and you're scratched for tonight's game," Coach tells me in the morning as we walk into the dining room for breakfast. "For your own good. I know you're banged up and exhausted. I don't want you to risk a more serious injury."

"No," I say hotly as anger courses through me. "I'm playing. I've scored every time we've played the Cryptid. We need the points for the standings. Liam, please, don't do this."

I almost never call Coach by his first name. It's not how we do things. We're friends, and he's going to be my brother-in-law, but we keep those connections out of the rink.

Sighing, he runs his hand through his hair and looks around, leading me out of the dining room and to a pair of chairs set in a relatively private area of the lobby. We sit in the dark brown leather chairs, facing each other. Coach leans forward and rests his elbows on his knees, his hands loosely clasped.

"Listen, Trev, I'm doing this for your own good. I see what's happening on the ice. You're being targeted."

"I can handle it."

"There's no doubt you're tough and will take whatever anyone dishes out. But we can't risk you suffering a season-ending injury because you're too stubborn to rest. We're off two days before our next game, and it's at home, so you're going to be able to sleep in your own bed instead of switching time zones constantly. You can heal. I know your ribs are aching. Are they cracked? Do you need to be seen by the team doctor?"

I shake my head. "No. I'm fine. So I'm going to sit up in the stands, twiddling my thumbs like an asshole? Who's taking my spot?"

"Moving Mac to center and Alvarez to first-line wing."

"Fucking dance show," I grumble. "This wouldn't be happening if you didn't force me to do it."

And I wouldn't have met Sophie. I guess this is what they mean by bittersweet. Her dream is killing mine. But I can't not help her reach hers. I need to do better. Keep my head on a swivel so I can avoid the hits on the ice. Pass the puck more. If I don't have the puck, they can't hit me.

I sense Sophie's presence as she enters the lobby. I smell her first —oranges and vanilla today. And before I can swivel in my chair to look for her, the hairs on the back of my neck stand up. My body knows when she's nearby. And then there she is, stepping off the elevator with her brother and Randi. My wolf is happier having her near, and I'm happy too. So damn happy to see her smiling. My heart aches. I feel guilty being so miserable doing something she loves. It's not that I don't enjoy dancing, I do. But I can't enjoy it while it's taking away time from the thing *I* love. If the show was during the summer, it'd be an entirely different situation. But it's not. So I have to make the best of the hand I've been dealt.

Coach and I join the others in the breakfast room, sitting with Randi, Mac, Daphne, Logan, and Sophie. I order juice and look over the menu. After placing our orders, Sophie touches my arm to get my attention. She's beaming.

"It's shifter week! We'll film an intro with us as our wolves that they'll show before we dance in the ballroom. The song we have is beautiful. I'd never heard it before. Oh, our style is contemporary ballroom, so we'll have some freedom. I'm so excited! Want to hear the song?"

She's bouncing in her seat, and the joy radiating off her is a punch to the solar plexus. I want her to be excited and happy doing what she loves, but I know this week will mean extra work filming as my wolf. I don't shift a lot during hockey season because it's strenuous. I tend to save it for when I have a few days off. And I'm not banged all to hell.

"Yeah," I say, trying to muster a smile. "Let's hear it."

Randi and Daphne are nodding eagerly. They love all the show stuff, all the peeks behind the scenes.

Sophie hits play, and the first notes shiver into the air—acoustic guitar with a light drumbeat. Daphne gasps as a female vocalist starts singing in a high, clear voice about a full moon rising and a whisper of a breeze.

"Sunshine, are you okay?" Logan asks as he gently brushes away a tear trailing down his wife's cheek. "Is it Birdie?"

She shakes her head no and gives a wobbly smile as Sophie hits pause on the song.

"I haven't heard that song in forever!" she says.

"You know it after that tiny bit?" Sophie asks. "I've never heard of it."

Daphne nods. "It's from the early 90s, Kathy Mattea. The song is called 'Asking Us to Dance.' It was my parents' favorite song. They'd dance to it in the kitchen when I was a little girl. It's been close to fifteen years since I've heard it." She sniffles and swallows hard. "Not since they died."

"Are you going to be okay?" I ask. Daphne's parents died in a car accident when she was a teenager, and I know the loss has been weighing heavily on her now that she's about to have a child.

Daphne's smile is brilliant. "Yes, absolutely! The night of the live show would've been their thirtieth wedding anniversary. They got pregnant with me their senior year of college and had a courthouse wedding. You guys dancing to that song is like a sign they're with me and Birdie."

Now we all have tears in our eyes.

"What is contemporary ballroom?" Randi asks, obviously trying to move us on to happier topics and regain composure. I'm glad she does. No one has danced it on the show yet.

"It's a mashup." Sophie smiles at me. "You're going to smash this, Trevor. I'm so excited. It's a mix of no-rules contemporary dance and elements of ballroom. So we can do lifts and leaps and then incorporate the Viennese waltz. I can picture it... It's going to be gorgeous. Can we start choreo after your practice? I know it's only an hour or so, but you'll get the contemporary part easily, and you know the basics of waltzing already."

The server delivering our meals buys me time in responding.

"I don't have practice today," I say before taking a bite of my spinach omelet.

"We don't?" Mac asks.

"*I don't,*" I say with emphasis. "Because I'm not playing tonight."

Randi gasps. Mac freezes with his teacup halfway to his lips.

Sophie gives an excited little clap. "You have the day off? So we can practice extra? Yay!"

I close my eyes and lower my head. Before I can say anything, Mac responds.

"Soph. He's not playing because he's hurt." Mac raises a brow and swings his eyes to mine. "Right? Coach is making you rest?"

I nod, afraid to look at Sophie. I don't want to see the anger or disappointment—or both—on her beautiful face. Especially since she's so excited.

It's like the entire dining room's gone silent. I open my eyes and look around, but no one is looking at me. They don't have to. They're shifters, and they can hear a blue jay fart two blocks away.

"Oh, Trevor," Sophie says sadly, taking my hand where it's resting on the table. "Why didn't you tell me?"

I give a slight shrug, mostly because a full one causes movement in my ribs and my left shoulder aches from hitting the glass last night. Swallowing the lump in my throat, I chance a glance at her. Her eyes are a darker blue than usual, and her brow is furrowed. I hate seeing worry clouding her expression.

"It's not a big deal, Soph. I'm sore. A couple days rest, and I'll be good as new."

Daphne points her fork at me. "You're getting hit like you're a piñata at a six-year-old's birthday party. You're a target. It's amazing you haven't been hurt more severely."

"Wait." Sophie focuses on Daphne. "They're hitting him on purpose? More than usual? Why?"

No one answers her, and everyone trains their eyes on their plates.

"Because of the show?" she asks.

Mac clears his throat. "Yeah. Some of our opponents are saying nasty shit to him and playing more physically than usual."

"Well, punch them. Aren't hockey fights a thing?" She curls her fingers into tiny fists like she's going to fight them on my behalf. I bet she would, given the opportunity.

Mac shakes his head. "We're not allowed to fight. We can be kicked out of the league. It's not like the human professional league. Every time Carter has the puck, he has a target on his back."

Sophie slams her tiny fist on the table. "Then stop passing him the puck!" She looks around like we're idiots for not thinking of that.

"My job is to get the puck and shoot it in the net. If I don't have the puck, there's no reason for me to be on the ice, and I may as well be figure skating." I rest my hand on her thigh so I don't strain my shoulder. Thankfully I can use my fingers to caress her without feeling pain. Her hand drops to mine, and she lightly runs her fingertips along the back of my hand. It's the barest of touches, but it's soothing a lot of my aches and pains.

"Can't you avoid them?" Her voice is husky, and tears glisten in her eyes.

"I can't play scared. That's a sure way to get hurt. I get hit. It's part of the game. I've been hit thousands of times. I've been playing since I was a kid. If you don't want to get hit, you shouldn't play in a professional league."

"So, quit the show," Sophie says quietly. "It's not worth it if you're going to get hurt because of it."

I look up to see Mac's eyes boring into me. I feel the weight of all my teammates' eyes on me. She's giving me an out. I can focus on hockey, and we can get back to playing more consistently.

It's tempting.

But I can't do it.

"No." I shake my head firmly. "I'm not quitting. I made a commitment, and I'm going to honor it. It's three more weeks. I can do it. But I'm taking a rest day today. We can start choreo when we get home tomorrow."

I don't look at my teammates to see what their opinions are. The gratitude and maybe something more shining in Sophie's eyes is all I need. I don't know if I'm making the right decision, but it's the only choice I can make.

15

SOPHIE

"Oh, Trevor," I say on an exhale as he takes off his shirt in our room. Normally those words are in appreciation of his sculpted muscles and smooth skin. This time it's in dismay. We undressed in the dark when we arrived early this morning, so this is my first glimpse at all the bruises painting his torso and shoulders. "How are they allowed to do this? That isn't nice."

"Honey, hockey isn't about being nice. It's about winning. If I'm an obstacle to them getting the puck into the goal, then they're going through me, and if I get bumps and bruises, so be it."

My heart trips when he calls me "honey." He's been doing it more often the past few weeks, and I don't know if he even realizes it. I know I slip sometimes and call him "baby" or use "boyo" as a term of endearment. It's been so easy being together. It's not feeling like a fling. It's feeling like...life. Like this is what our life could be like for years to come. I know his slips of the tongue don't mean anything, but for a moment, I can pretend we have a real relationship and not something with an expiration date. In the weeks we've been no-strings sleeping with each other, I've begun to see what having a true partner is like. And I've begun to ache for one. It terrifies me. Because

it's not just any old someone I'm aching for. It's Trevor. I want a partner, I want to be in love, but I don't want to hurt anyone, and the
things I want and don't want will only hurt a man like Trevor. Trevor
in pain, physical or emotional, is the last thing I want. If only he
wasn't who and what he is. But if he was any different, I don't know
that I'd feel as deeply as I do for him. I wish I wasn't who and what I
am, but trying to change would only lead to unhappiness for us both.
Still, I can dream. But not now. Right now, the priority is Trevor and
him being healthy and safe while playing hockey.

"It's more than that. They're trying to hurt you. It's not about
scoring, it's about injuring you. They're talking about me to get to
you. Not just you, but my brother too."

My brother doesn't have a temper. Even when we were kids, he
was the one that always played fairly. But he's protective as the day
is long, and if someone's speaking badly about me, he'll settle it. A
flush creeps up Trevor's neck and along the sexy stubble dusting his
cheeks. He takes my hand and pulls me into his embrace. I want to
snuggle in and hold on tight, but I'm afraid of hurting him.

"It doesn't matter what he said." Trevor nuzzles the top of my
head with his nose. "Chirping is part of the game. We're profes-
sionals and should tune it out."

"But you're not. Dec isn't. He reacted, and then it all came down
on you. I can't risk you getting hurt."

He slips his calloused palm under my T-shirt and runs it up and
down my back. If I was a cat shifter, I'd be purring.

"I'm healing up. I'll be fine to start learning this week's dance
tomorrow."

I growl in frustration. "I don't care about the dance, I care about
you!"

His hand stills, and we stand there in stunned silence. I can't
believe I said that, but I meant it. And I'm petrified. Dancing is
what's most important to me. No man, especially not *this* man, can
shift my focus. I won't fall into the trap my mother did. But I am falling. And savoring every second.

"It's okay, Sophie, I know what you meant," Trevor says, pressing a kiss to the crown of my head. "You're sweet. I'm tough. I'll heal up the next couple of days and be as good as new. I can give as good as I get, don't worry."

Letting out a giggle I don't really feel to try and lighten the mood, I joke, "I know that, boyo. But I don't want you to risk injury on the ice because you're dancing and the other teams are full of assholes."

I step out of his hold, wrapping my arms around my stomach. "Do you harass the players on the other teams who are doing the shows?"

He shrugs. "No, but our show started first, and since you're Mac's sister, it's a two-for-one chirp to piss us off."

"Woo-hoo for efficiency," I mutter.

Trevor laughs and then groans, clutching his ribs. "Sophie, you can't make me laugh until tomorrow when I've healed up some more."

"What are you going to do today? You can't practice. Are you going to sleep? Want to play tourist?"

He shakes his head. "I'm going to watch video with the team and observe practice. Maybe I'll see things to fix since I'm not on the ice and involved in the play. Mac picked up a weakness on our left side none of us caught because he was sitting out with his broken hand. I'm praying I'll see something simple to fix to stop us from losing so many games. We're dropping in the standings. At this point, we'll be lucky to play for a wild card spot, when a month ago, we were the top seed in our division." He jams his fingers in his thick copper-tinged hair and tugs it in frustration. "We're falling apart, and it doesn't make sense."

But it does. First the team captain falls in love. Then Dec and Miranda have all their drama. Now we're having a fling. Three of the team's top players are distracted with romance. Well, in our case— sex. They lost their focus on hockey. That's why they aren't playing as well as they were.

I knew it would happen. That's why I can't let whatever feelings I may have for Trevor distract me from my goals. I'm not going to end up like my mother or my brother, letting love keep me from my dreams. No point in sharing my theory. It's not like Declan and Miranda would break up to help the Devil Birds win games. Declan would stop playing hockey before he left the woman he loves.

"What's your plan? Do you want to watch practice?" Trevor asks.

"Um...no. It's enough to watch the games. I don't need to see practice. No one wants to see how the sausage is made, Trevor."

His chuckle is light in deference to his aching ribs, but it still warms me.

"I'm going to start choreographing our shifter dance. Do you think you'll be okay to do lifts?"

He runs a calloused finger along my forearm, bringing out goose-bumps. The way he wiggles his brows above his hazel eyes makes me smile softly as my tummy flips.

"By tomorrow, I'm going to be healed up enough to do all sorts of things, Sophie. If you were on top, we could do stuff now."

I roll my eyes and give him a gentle pat on his stubbled cheek.

"Keep dreaming, boyo. If you're too banged up to dance, you're too banged up to do other things."

His low groan as I grab my laptop and settle on the recliner in the room almost makes me feel guilty. Almost. Before I can hit play to start our song, he leans over my laptop and kisses me sweetly. I whimper when he pulls away before I have a chance to deepen our kiss. Even if we can't do other things today, kissing is still on the menu.

"I'm gonna go hang out with the team for video and then go to the rink for practice. Have fun." He taps me on the tip of my nose as he straightens.

It's silly how that tiny gesture sets butterflies alight throughout my nervous system. My smile is probably dreamy as I look up at him. "Okay. I hope you see stuff that can help. Take care."

We look at each other, and I feel like there are so many other things being said, but neither one of us will voice them. I'm refusing to even acknowledge what they are. It may as well be static on an old radio.

I hit play on my phone as the door clicks closed behind him. The first couple of times I listen to the song, I sit with my eyes shut and let the music wash over me. I lose myself in the crests and dips of the melody. Then I start counting the beats and making notes of movements that could work there. Sometimes I jump right into choreographing a piece and just move to the music. But sometimes, like now, I outline the dance before starting to move. Almost like what I imagine authors do before starting a novel.

Soon the urge to move is irresistible, and I start freestyling to the music. With Trevor's contemporary skills and his incredible strength, he's going to shine in this dance. We'll be able to do lifts. I'm excited by that but also nervous. I've done lifts before, but never with a partner with his strength and experience. Ian is the only shifter partner I've had, but our lifts were limited and, frankly, fairly tame. With Trevor's cheerleading experience, he'll be able to do just about anything I ask of him. I'm eager to see what we can come up with, but I'm worried I won't be good enough to match him. That's the theme with us—I can't match what he needs. But maybe for this week, we can give each other what's necessary to move closer to both of our dreams coming true. We only need to get through three more weeks, and then the show will be over. I'll either be a pro on the show, or I'll be finding a new partner and hitting the competition circuit again. No matter what, my fling with Trevor will be over, and I'll have to get used to being alone again. It's not even about the sex, as incredible as *that* is. I've enjoyed being with him in a way I've never experienced with another man.

I would give anything to be a different kind of woman and want to be the sort of wife and mother a man like Trevor expects in his mate. To be a woman like my mother. But I know I can't, and I'm not going to doom either of us to a lifetime of unhappiness and regret when I can't live up to the role I'd be put in. It wouldn't be fair to either of us. Why must life be such a bitch sometimes?

I'm sitting with Daphne and Miranda in a box at the Cryptids' arena, watching the teams warm up on the ice. Trevor sits at a table farther back in the box with Jake.

"I love visiting Colorado Springs," Daphne says, "but being over a mile above sea level with the thinner air is rough. No matter how fit our Devil Birds are, it's always a challenge to play here."

"Does the Colorado team have an advantage at lower altitudes? More stamina?" I munch on the handful of popcorn I grabbed out of the communal tub we're sharing. Daphne mixed in colorful chocolates and peanut butter candies, and the combination of flavors is making my taste buds happy. I'm glad Daphne mentioned the altitude. I thought I was being lazy, getting tired while working on movements for our dance this week. I'm relieved to know it's normal.

She shrugs. "Maybe a slight advantage in conditioning, but not enough to make a difference. Being at sea level isn't as much of an advantage for the high-altitude teams, especially with everyone being so highly conditioned in general. And since everyone is a shifter, they acclimate more quickly anyway. They don't need days like a human does before exerting themselves. Just staying overnight seems to be enough for them to be good to go."

"Does altitude affect avian shifters like Bridget or Logan?" The Devil Birds' goalie is a goose shifter, but that's not common knowledge, and Daphne's husband is an eagle shifter. I've always been curious about that, but I grew up surrounded by wolf shifters and didn't have anyone to ask.

"No, they acclimate easily. Of course, Logan is used to traveling, so things like altitude and time zones don't affect him that much. How is Trevor doing? I'm glad they aren't playing him tonight. All the healing he has to do, plus the altitude? I don't know how he'd get through a full game. He'd be like a limping deer hunted by a ravenous pack of wolves." She grimaces and shoots me an apologetic glance. "No offense."

I chuckle. "None taken."

The last thing I want is for Trevor to not be able to perform at full strength and speed. Playing hurt is risking greater injury, and we can't have that. Glancing over my shoulder at Trevor, I watch him nod while listening earnestly to Jake, who's pointing at something on the ice. Trevor's brow furrows as he shakes his head. I hear the word "trade," but nothing else of their conversation because they're speaking quietly and the Cryptids' arena is loud.

Grabbing Miranda's arm, I nervously ask, "Trevor isn't getting traded, is he?"

It would devastate him to leave the team. I'm not sure he'd play for another one. As much as he loves playing professional hockey, he loves playing in his hometown and working with his friends. I'll dance anywhere to achieve my goals, but Trevor is more selective. His goals stretch far beyond playing hockey. Dance is all I have.

Miranda shakes her head emphatically. "No! Why would you think that? Has Trevor said anything about wanting to play elsewhere?" It's her turn to glance over her shoulder to where Trevor and Jake are seated.

"No, we haven't talked about the trade deadline at all. But I know it's coming up and it's been on everyone's mind. Will anyone be traded from the team?"

Miranda chews on her cheek. "I can't say anything. There have been discussions, and maybe there will be some new faces in the locker room and folks moving on, but nothing is definite, and it wouldn't be anyone at the barn. I can't say anything more than that. I shouldn't have even said that much."

We settle in to watch the game. Declan's playing Trevor's usual position and is doing a fine job. The team seems to be working well together. It's a physical game but not to the level it has been recently, and no one player seems to be targeted like Trevor has been. It's almost like there's a bounty on his head. I'm even more glad he's sitting this game out. The team heads off the ice after a scoreless first period, and I join Trevor. He's scrolling through his phone and gives me the briefest glance when I rest my hand on his shoulder.

"Hey." I lean into him.

He stiffens and leans away, shrugging his shoulder to dislodge my hand. "There could be cameras."

I look around. The box is visible from around the arena, but I don't notice anyone paying any particular attention to us. The announcers are across the ice from us, but they're chatting with each other for their intermission report.

"So? We're on camera all the time."

"For dancing, yeah, but if they see us cuddling up here, that'll fan the flames of the rumors that we're dating."

I know we're not public, but I didn't realize we were a secret.

"Right. Sorry." I step away and dodge his hand when he reaches out for me.

"Soph..." he says on a sigh. "I'm sorry. The hockey blogs are saying you're the reason my game has been crap and the team has been losing. I know that's not true. The team knows it's not true. But I don't want to give anyone ammunition to talk crap about you. I can't stand it."

I swallow down the lump that's clogging my throat. "No worries, Trevor. I get it. You all need to be focused on getting the playoffs and not dealing with ridiculous rumors about us being in a relationship. In three weeks, I'll be gone, and all the drama stirred up will be proven false. It's all good."

I keep my spine straight as I walk to the bathroom conveniently located in our box. Resting my back against the locked door, I allow myself the indulgence of a few tears before I lock down my heart, take care of business, and prepare to emerge like I don't have a concern in the world. I'm a dancer and an actress. If I was able to carry a tune, I could market myself as a triple threat. But I can't, so I better make sure I stay focused on being the best dancer I can be.

16

TREVOR

THE DEVIL BIRDS WON. I DIDN'T PLAY, AND THEY WON. MAC HAD A HAT trick. Alvarez was great on the first line. The guy brought up from the Demon Geese got an assist to earn his first point in the PHL. Everyone had a great game. Because I wasn't on the ice. I wasn't a distraction. No one had to step up to prevent me from becoming roadkill, so they could focus on getting the puck in the net.

Am I being selfish wanting to play professional hockey? Maybe I'd help the team more by not being on the roster.

"Stop it," Mac says in his deep Scottish brogue. We're sitting together on the flight home from Colorado. Sophie and Randi are huddled together across the aisle, giggling over something Randi has pulled up on her phone.

"Stop what?" I ask, looking first at him and then across the table to Bedard and Stone. We're playing the card game Uno and Bedard just hit Stone with a draw two card.

"Thinking you're not good enough and shouldn't be on the team. Don't be daft. You're necessary. You belong. You not being on the ice didn't help us win tonight. Our losses aren't because of you. Hockey is a team sport."

We joke about Mac being able to read minds, and he swears he can't, but it's spooky how much he knows.

"Yeah, but..."

"No," Mac says firmly. "You start thinking this shit and it's going to screw you up. Everyone hits rough patches. There's a bunch of shit hitting the fan all at once—trying to make the playoffs, you having to compete on the dance show, me and Bedard getting into relationships..."

I'm startled when he says this. Shocked when Bedard nods in agreement.

"Dude," our team captain says, "it's not just you dealing with changes and worrying it's affecting your game. You also have the other teams placing a bounty on you. They aren't doing that because you're dancing with Sophie. They're doing it because you are so important to us on the ice and how it'll impact us if you aren't playing."

I swallow thickly. It's nice to hear these words from my teammates, men I respect and care about.

"But..." I say again.

"But we are a team," Bedard says insistently, with Stone nodding in agreement. "Our success does not rest solely on your shoulders. As important as you are, everyone is important. We all have our roles. And we've all slipped sometime during the season. It's a shit show when it's a bunch of us at once, but that's not your fault. You're not getting any time off. When you're not skating, you're dancing. You're doing everything you can. Give yourself a break."

I appreciate his kindness, but I'm not dancing for me, I'm dancing for Sophie. I can't let temporary weakness undo what Sophie's been working toward for a lifetime. Nodding, I throw a card down on the pile to move the game along.

Waking in my own bed with Sophie in my arms is a heaven I never knew existed. We arrived home at dawn and fell into bed. I'm going to miss the peace I find holding Sophie. Hockey doesn't press sleepy kisses on my pec or wear the cutest pink plastic eyeglasses I've ever seen. Swallowing the lump that forms in my throat whenever I think about my time with Sophie ending, I press a kiss to the crown of her strawberry-scented hair.

"Hmm..." She nuzzles into my chest. "Good morning."

"Did you sleep okay?"

She answers me by snuggling deeper under my covers and running her toes along my calf. I yelp because they're like five little ice cubes against my skin. Her giggle isn't like tinkling bells. It's like an asthmatic piglet and that makes me laugh as I wrap her in my arms and roll on top of her. Gone is the sleepiness in her ocean-blue eyes. All I see now is hunger.

Brushing her hair off her forehead, I run my fingertips down the side of her face. "You are so beautiful."

Her impish grin invites me to kiss the corner of it. "You're okay, I guess, boyo," she teases. "Are you okay?"

I press my hard cock against her center. "You tell me."

She smirks and raises her hips to rub against me. "That part working was never a question. How are your ribs and other bits?"

"Sophie, everything's working as it should be. I think limbering up before we start dancing is a good thing, don't you?"

Her low, sexy chuckle rubs her tank-top-covered breasts against my bare chest with delicious friction. I start kissing behind her ear— that always makes her gasp. When I reach the spot where her neck and shoulder meet, the urge to give her a mate mark is overwhelming. It's what wolf shifters in the old days did to claim their mate, but modern wolf shifters don't do it anymore. Even if we did, I can't do it. I can't claim a mate, especially not Sophie. It wouldn't be fair to Sophie to claim her as my mate when I can't give her what any female wolf shifter would want for her life.

My desire to make love to her is still there. It's always going to be there as long as I live. But I can't right now. It's going to reveal too much of my heart, and I can't do it. I give her neck the tiniest nip as a salve to my soul before rolling away.

"Sorry," I say. "I can hear Mac and Miranda moving around, and it's just weird."

Sophie props up on her elbow and looks down on my face with a furrowed brow.

"You better not start getting performance anxiety on the dance floor too, Trevor."

I roll my eyes. "Your brother has been watching us dance for weeks. I'm used to that. But I don't think *this* brother wants to hear us boinking, and I don't want to have to look him in the eye over a plate of eggs, knowing the delicious things I just did to his little sister with him in earshot. It's a respect thing as much as it's a self-preservation thing."

With a big sigh, Sophie rises from the bed, giving me a great view of her pert ass cheeks peeking out from the little shorts she wears to sleep in. I almost regret the slight fib I just told. I don't want Mac to hear what we do, but I added extra soundproofing to my room when I was renovating the apartments, so they'd have to be pressing their ears up to the door to hear anything. But I can't trust myself to make love with Sophie and not claim her. Not this morning.

She dresses in dance clothes then pulls joggers and a T-shirt out of my dresser and tosses them at me.

As my head emerges from my shirt, I ask, "Are we practicing here, or do we have to be filmed?"

"Practicing here and being filmed. Logan is going to help us. Tonight's the full moon, so if we can get the part of our dance in shifter form filmed tonight, it'll be awesome."

Sophie walks to the window overlooking the field between the barn and the trees. "Can we use the field?"

I walk to her and wrap my arms around her from behind. When she leans back and turns her face up to mine, I bend my head and press a tender kiss to her lips.

"Anything you want, Princess. If I can give it to you, I will."

It must be my imagination that a mix of sadness and longing flashes in her blue eyes. She can't want anything from me—she's been insistent that what we have remains a fling. I don't blame her.

We leave my room and find everyone sharing eggs and pancakes in the common kitchen. That's a nice thing about being shifters—we burn calories so efficiently that we can enjoy things like pancakes or waffles and not be cheating on a nutrition plan like our human hockey league counterparts. We do have to pay attention to nutrition, of course, but we enjoy flexibility too.

"You're starting the choreography for the shifter week dance today?" Miranda asks, dropping marshmallows into her hot chocolate.

Sophie holds out her mug for Miranda to drop some into hers too. Neither one of them is back to drinking tea yet. "Yeah, Logan agreed to film us so we can use the footage for the opening of our dance on the show. With the full moon and it being a clear night, it's too perfect to pass up."

Sophie's fur is lustrous in the moonlight. If I didn't know better, I'd think she sprayed glitter to give her an extra sparkle, but it's all Sophie. The contrast between my dark fur and her silvery strands is striking. She jokes about her wolf being decorative due to poor eyesight, but I could never find fault with a creature so stunning.

We spent the morning working on this portion of our dance. Normally we use counts, but since we can't speak in wolf form unless we yip or howl, Logan is playing the track on his phone. It will be dubbed into the final version to cut out any of the crunching our paws make on the frozen field we're dancing in.

Taking our spots across the field from each other, I fix my gaze on Sophie. She's looking in my direction, but she can't see clearly enough to view my expression. Is Logan's camera picking up the way

I look at Sophie? It's like she hung the moon resting heavily in the sky.

"Five, four, three..." Mallory counts us down as she starts the song. Logan is in his golden eagle form and using a specialty camera so he can film us aerially. The dreamy notes of a guitar with a steady drumbeat carry across the field as Sophie and I start our measured advance toward each other, meeting in the center of the field in a stream of moonlight. We move so we're side by side, facing in opposite directions, and then circle counterclockwise. With the stark difference in our coloring, we're almost a furry yin and yang symbol as our bodies curve. Logan glides above us, his massive wingspan carrying him silently.

After our circle together, I continue around Sophie until we're side by side again. We turn our heads and nuzzle each other in greeting and affection. I sneak a playful nip in along her jaw, my wolf's teeth so close to that place he wants so badly. I can feel the need pulsing in him. *Claim her.* I can't. He'll have to be satisfied with a nip. Her crystal blue eyes, stunning against the pewter-colored fur surrounding them, widen in surprise, but she doesn't miss a step. We stride in tandem toward the treeline, entwining our tails as if we're holding hands.

I'm certain we got it in one take, but we do it a few more times so Logan can edit if necessary. We gather in the main room of the barn to watch the rough footage. Daphne is rubbing her eyes as she sits up on the sofa where she'd been taking a nap. Logan gives her a cuddle and rubs her baby bump before queuing up the footage. Pretty sure we all gasp when we realize what Logan's camera captured. What I'd imagined we would look like pales in comparison to what's on the screen. We can faintly hear the track in the background, and it confirms that we're hitting the beat as we approach each other. I'm holding Sophie's hand as we watch, as if it's the most natural thing in the world to do. And to me, it is.

The silence in the ballroom is deafening as Sophie and I walk toward the judges hand in hand. There's a flicker of panic in her eyes when she looks up at me, and I squeeze her hand in reassurance. She has nothing to worry about because the applause is thundering when it comes. Her smile is brighter than all the studio lights put together when she hugs me. I lift and spin her as we reach Ian where he's standing before the judges' table. The audience is on their feet, joined by Carlo and Mary Ann. She's wiping away a tear. Glen isn't standing, but he's applauding and nodding approvingly. He motions for the crowd to sit and quiet down, and when they do, he bestows us with one of his rare smiles.

"Very well done, you two. You were stunning in your wolf forms, and the videography for that outdoor sequence was magical. The way you mixed the lifts of contemporary dancing with the classic Viennese waltz was lovely. Trevor, your experience as a cheerleader and your obvious strength created spectacular moments, but you were always in control and Sophie seemed perfectly at ease. Have you ever done lifts and tosses like that, Sophie?"

I look down at her and meet her eyes. She kept pushing me to throw her higher and make our lifts more complex because she wanted to feel what it was like to fly. The trust she put in me is humbling.

"No, Glen, I haven't. It was incredible. I wouldn't trust anyone other than Trevor to do some of those moves. I knew he wouldn't let me fall."

She's right, I would never let her fall. But that hasn't stopped me from falling for her.

"I could see how seriously he was taking it. Trevor, you danced beautifully, but we could see on your face how much you were thinking about everything. You can do this, your body knows what to do, now get your face following the program. No more stress or worry, look like you're enjoying yourself."

Mary Ann wipes away a tear before giving us praise. Carlo just shrugs and starts clapping again. We get our first tens from Mary

Ann and Carlo, but Glen is stingy and gives us a nine. From what I hear, a ten from Glen is a rarity, but I'm determined to earn one for Sophie. She deserves it. We'll get tens across the board next week in the semifinals. If I can't give us a future, at least I can give Sophie the tens she deserves.

17
TREVOR

THIS WEEK HAS BEEN CRAZY. WE'RE PREPARING FOR THE SEMIFINALS AND ARE dancing the jive. It's an up-tempo dance with lots of kicks, flicks, and rock steps. We're supposed to be connected to each other but also show joy and engage the audience. There are spins, kicks, and lifts. It's very technical. I'm trying the best I can to learn everything, but my brain is muddled. The dance steps are competing with new hockey plays we're trying to keep us in the wild card race for the playoffs. The string of losses these past few weeks has dropped our standing so much we're scrambling to earn the spot in the Dickinson Cup playoffs that was ours all season long. Everyone says hockey is a team sport, but I feel like it's my fault we've been slipping down the rankings like a penguin sliding down an iceberg.

Sophie is at her place in Zoom meetings with the producers, so I snag Randi to help me practice downstairs. Randi's trying to help me get the dance into my brain well enough that muscle memory takes over, so I can focus on looking like I'm having fun and not trying to remember what my arms and legs need to do.

I want to prove to Sophie I can do this and that I'm willing to do whatever I have to, even if that means giving cheesy smiles and acting like I don't have two tons of stress on my shoulders. I can fake anything for ninety seconds. I have the moves down, at least most of the time. Okay, some of the time. It's my expression that's the real problem. I can't just let go and dance. I think about every step and how important this is to Sophie, and it's messing with my head, causing me to miss steps. And all of that's showing on my face. I know Sophie's frustrated and trying to not show it. In a way, that makes me feel worse. I'm failing her like I'm failing my team. I've never failed anything before, and now is a lousy time to become an expert at it.

"You know the steps, Trev, what's the problem?" Randi asks after she watches the video of our last run-through.

I point to my face. "This."

She lays a gentle hand on my forearm and gives me a sympathetic look. "Trevor, you can't help that you're ugly. You have a great personality that makes up for it."

My arm whips out to pull her against me, and I give her a noogie on her head. She squirms and giggles until I release her.

When she catches her breath, she pins me with her clear gray gaze. "If you want to dance with joy, you need to feel it. What makes you happy? You don't have to tell me, just think of that while you're dancing."

The only thing I can think of is Sophie. She brings me joy, and this time when I move into the choreography for the jive with Randi, I feel that joy in my limbs, imagining Sophie beside me dancing, imagining me giving her everything she wants and needs. Imagining I have the power to make her happy.

It works. I can feel it, and I can see it in Randi's expression. I'm giving Randi a high five when I glimpse Sophie in the studio mirror. She's backing away like she doesn't want me to see her. Crap. I didn't want her to know I was practicing with Randi. I don't want the stress of my failures on her shoulders. So I lied. I told her I had extra on-ice practice this morning so I could work with Randi. I feel like I'm cheating on Sophie. I may be a lot of things, but I've never been a cheater. Great. I can't even get being in a fling right.

18

SOPHIE

I watch Trevor and Miranda dance through my choreography. We have the jive for our quarterfinal, and Trevor hasn't been able to get it right, no matter how many times we've practiced the steps. It's not even one consistent step that I can change to make it easier. He does something different incorrectly each time. It's impossible to know what to fix. But here he is, dancing it perfectly with Miranda. Maybe it's my fault. Maybe I'm not a good enough partner for him. I wasn't a good enough partner for Ian. I've never been able to keep a partner —in dance or in life.

I back away before they notice me, but I guess I wasn't fast enough because Trevor calls out my name and rushes after me. Hurriedly brushing the tears off my cheeks, I keep my back to him. Damn. When did I start crying?

"Sophie, what's wrong?"

When I don't turn around, he scoots around in front of me. I keep my head lowered because I don't want him to see the streaks of my tears or my red-rimmed eyes.

"Hey," he says softly, putting a finger under my chin to gently raise my face to his. "What's wrong? Why are you crying?"

Jerking my head away, I take a step back. He suddenly feels way too close. "All the times we practice that dance, and you can't get it right. Now you're dancing with Miranda and suddenly, you're perfect? Why can you dance with her and not with me? Do you hate dancing with me that much?" I know I sound angry. I'm glad for it. Anger is a trusty costume, hiding how I really feel. It's my default, so people don't know my vulnerabilities.

A beautiful smile spreads across his face, and it makes my heart ache. "I was doing it right? Really?"

I give a single stiff nod. "Yes, you had all the steps. You were perfectly in rhythm. Your form was great, and you looked like you were having fun. Fun you don't have when we dance together. I'm a horrible teacher and a horrible partner, and I'm sorry you're stuck with me."

My attempt to step around him is thwarted when he gently grabs me by my arms and pulls me in for a hug. I stand stiff in his embrace as long as I can, but I eventually relax and rest against him, hooking my fingers on the belt loops of the jeans resting on his trim hips. His usual scent of pine and man, mixed with the slightest tinge of sweat earned dancing, is intoxicating. It takes so much strength to not go up on tiptoe and kiss the base of his throat.

He presses a kiss to the top of my head and tightens his arms around me. His sigh as he rests his cheek on my hair is so deep, I can feel his chest rise and fall.

"Sophie, it's...it's easy to dance with Miranda. I know exactly how she's going to move, and her body just feels right in my arms because we've worked together for *years*. But I was thinking of you. I'm always thinking of you."

Of course, perfect Miranda is doing perfect Miranda things again. I try to pull out of his embrace, but he just tightens his hold—not in a restrictive way, but more in a *please don't leave me* way that stops my flight.

"Stop, just listen to me," he pleads, leaning back to see my face.

"Miranda is easy to dance with because she's comfortable. She's like old ratty sweatpants."

"Hey!" I hear from the studio, and it makes me giggle.

"Turn off your ears or turn up the music, Randi! This is private!" Trevor calls back. Suddenly an old song from the Irish band The Corrs plays at a high volume. I haven't heard it in years, and it makes me sad. I love that song.

Trevor looks back down at me. "As I was saying, dancing with Miranda is comfortable. You make me nervous. I want to be perfect for you, and it's extremely hard to concentrate on the steps and the rhythm and everything else that goes into it when I'm too distracted to learn."

My shoulders sag. I knew it. I'm a horrible teacher.

"I can't focus on learning the dance because I'm trying so hard not to kiss you. I can't count the steps because I'm counting the freckles on your adorable nose. When you're in my arms, everything I know flies out the window. Dancing with Miranda is easy. I'm not attracted to her. With you, I'm so busy fighting my attraction that I can't relax enough to perform. I'm a horrible student. I'm sorry."

Oh, my heart. This man. I wish I was a different person so I could try to keep him as my own. But I need to be true to myself or else I'll only hurt both of us.

"Trevor, you're not! You're wonderful. I wouldn't want to do this with anyone but you. I'm just sorry there's so much stress on you. The playoffs, the hockey semifinals, and finals of the show." *Us.* "It's a lot. And I know I'm demanding, which adds to your stress. You love to dance, and I'm ruining it for you."

He lowers his lips to mine and gives me the sweetest, tenderest kiss. I love our passionate kisses, full of fire and heat. But these kisses are precious to me and what I'll remember and cherish forever.

"Sophie, you aren't ruining anything for me. You make things better. These weeks with you have been wonderful. We just need to get through two more shows, and then you'll have the pro career you've been dreaming of. I can tough it out for a week and a half. I know the dance, so now I'll focus on smiling and engaging. We can do this, Soph, I know it."

I want to believe him.

Second to last dress rehearsal. I hate that I'm not measuring time by how many more dances I get with Trevor. The Devil Birds had their first game of the wild card round last night and lost. It's a round of five games total, and the first team to win three games advances to the playoffs for the Dickinson Cup. I know Trevor is kicking himself because he whiffed on a slapshot that would've tied the game and sent them to overtime. Instead, the New York team took control of the puck and got a goal past Brick, cementing their lead. He refuses to listen to anyone who says it wasn't his fault. As much as it's his job to make goals, it's Brick's job to stop them. If he's not blaming her, then he can't blame himself. But of course, the silly man doesn't see it that way.

We're dancing the jive to the theme song from an 80s movie full of dancing high school students. Growing up in Ireland and Scotland, I didn't experience proms and homecoming games like they do here in America. I'm in a flirty dress dripping with gold fringe, and Trevor looks like the All-American football quarterback in blue jeans, a white T-shirt, black high-top sneakers, and a letterman jacket. I bet he broke a lot of hearts in high school and college. Mine is breaking now, but it's my own fault.

He squeezes my hand and smiles down at me. "Ready?"

Nodding, we take our place on the stage for our dress rehearsal. We've already gone through notes for blocking, so we just need to do a full run-through of our routine and prepare for the live show. I love this routine. It shows off Trevor's athleticism and lets him use some of his skills from when he was a cheerleader. I know the crowd is going to go wild when they see him do a backflip off the judges' table to join me back on the dance floor before our last moves. We're in sync throughout, and Trevor's having fun. If the show tonight goes as well as the rehearsal is going, we're going to win. His flip goes perfectly, and we stand back-to-back and link arms for our final trick. Trevor leans forward at the waist so I'm resting on his back, and I flip over and land on my feet then immediately sit so I can slide through his legs to hit my final pose. We've done this dozens of times with no problem. This time, however, my left ankle twists, and it's less a graceful sit on the floor and more of a flop. I hiss, "Keep dancing!" and Trevor blessedly does. We hit our final poses and I'm smiling, but Trevor is looking at me with concern.

My ankle is slightly tweaked. A bit of ice and some painkillers, and I'll be right as rain for tonight. I believe that, I truly do. Until I go to stand and crumple to the floor, crying out from the pain shooting up my leg.

"Sophie!" both Ian and Trevor shout, rushing to my side. Ian immediately goes to my ankle, recognizing my injury in a flash. He gently grasps my foot.

"Oh, Soph," he says sadly. I see what he sees—my ankle is already swelling around the strap of my gold high-heeled dance shoe.

"It's fine," I say desperately as the medical team arrives. Trevor has taken my hand and refuses to move out of the way. "Just wrap it up good and tight, put some ice on it, and give me painkillers. I can do it."

An involuntary yelp slips out when Marvin, the show's medical officer, takes my foot in a gentle, yet firm grasp and unbuckles my shoe.

He shakes his head sadly. "Sophie, we've got to get this x-rayed. Best-case scenario, it's just a sprain, but there's no way you're dancing tonight."

The producers are here with camera people shooting every

moment of my dream dying. I'm a Mackenzie. I'm a proud and strong female wolf shifter. I'm not going to break down sobbing, asking, "Why me?" even though that's what I want to do.

"Let's get you back to the exam room and figure out what we're working with," Marvin says. "Ian, can you carry her?"

"Been doing it all my life." He's trying to make me laugh, I know that, so I smile weakly in response. Trevor looks like he wants to protest and carry me himself but doesn't want to delay me getting the treatment I need. It's just as well. If I was in Trevor's arms, I'd break down.

Ian places me on the exam table, and Marvin shoos everyone out.

"Can Trevor stay?" I ask, reaching out for his hand. He takes mine and raises it to his lips. He's been quiet, but I can see the concern shining from his eyes. Or maybe it's tears? Could be both.

Marvin nods. "Okay with me."

In my effort to not flinch, I squeeze Trevor's hand so hard he's the one flinching as Marvin examines my ankle. After some mmms and hmms and nods, Marvin looks up and gives me a slight smile. "You have a nasty sprain. I know you're a shifter and should heal quickly, but I can't medically clear you to dance tonight."

"I'll sign waivers. Whatever you want. I must dance tonight." Tears are streaming down my cheeks now. "Trevor, tell him. We've worked too hard. You've worked too hard to not dance."

Trevor brushes away my tears, but more follow their path. "Sophie, you can't risk injuring yourself worse. We need to let this heal properly so you can dance for the long haul. You can't throw away your future for one night."

Before I can protest further, Nancy and other producers come into the room. The smirk she gives me tanks any hope I have.

"Oh, Sophie," she says, her voice dripping in insincerity. "What a shame you can't dance tonight. Guess you'll have to drop out, Trevor."

Geoffrey, the head producer, gives me a sympathetic smile. I like

Geoffrey. "Not necessarily, Nancy. We can have another dancer substitute for you, Sophie. We have your rehearsal recorded, so one of the previously dismissed pros could learn it and dance with Trevor tonight. If Trevor isn't voted out and makes it to the finals, and you're medically cleared, then the two of you can compete next week."

"I don't want to dance with another pro," Trevor says.

"Then you can drop out," Nancy says.

Indecision flits across Trevor's face. His life would be easier without the stress and commitment of the show hanging over him.

Swallowing hard, I hope my smile is convincing. "It's okay, Trevor, whatever you decide to do. I know you're busy with the wild card games. Do what's best for you."

"Getting you to the finals is best for me," he says, running a fingertip down my nose and giving it a teasing bop. Turning to Geoffrey, he says, "I want to dance, but I have a suggestion for my partner. She knows the dance and would be great on the show. She's here in New York and can be at the studio within the hour."

"Yeah," I say, nodding slowly when I realize what he's suggesting. If I can't do this with him, there's no one else I'd rather he dance with.

"Who?" Nancy asks suspiciously.

"Randi Quinn," Trevor says. "She was my cheerleading stunt partner in college. She's the only person other than Sophie I'll dance with tonight. Can we show you what we can do, and you decide? If we don't meet your standards, then I'll drop out of the competition."

Geoffrey shrugs. "If she can get here quickly, we'll do what we can. Are you sure you don't want to work with another pro? They're your best chance, especially if you're doing this for Sophie's benefit."

"I'm sure," Trevor says confidently while texting. A smile crosses his face. "She'll be here in half an hour."

Nodding, I do my best to smile and be happy. He deserves the chance to show off the hard work he's done, and if he was going to perform any dance with Randi on the show, the jive is the one it should be. It fits the style of dance they do together perfectly, and it'll show off the trust and connection they've built over their years of cheering together. I know they're doing this to help me, but that doesn't stem the jealous voice in my head—the one that sounds like Doreen—telling me that, once again, Miranda's getting what should be mine. Shut the fuck up, Doreen.

19
TREVOR

RANDI JUMPS INTO MY ARMS, LAUGHING, AND I SPIN HER AROUND.

"We did it!" she yells, hugging me as I walk us over to where Ian stands near the judges' table.

We just danced the jive in the semifinal round, and it's up to the judges and the audience to decide if we were good enough to send me and Sophie through to next week's finals.

Carlo is standing, giving us his slow clap of approval. All the judges are smiling.

"Finally! You look like you're enjoying yourself, Trevor! We've been waiting to see that all season. It's a shame it's under these circumstances."

Nope, not answering that. I leave Randi with Ian and jog across the dance floor to where Sophie is sitting next to Declan. She's smiling, but I can see the strain behind it. Some of it has to be physical pain, but I know how badly she wishes she was there on the floor. I scoop her up in my arms and walk back to Ian and Randi. Cheers echo throughout the ballroom. Sophie tucks her face against my neck for a moment before lifting her head and waving to the crowd.

"How's your ankle, Sophie?" Glen asks.

"Sore and swollen," Sophie says with a grimace. "But fingers crossed I'll get to show it's healed in next week's finals."

"So what did you think of Trevor and Miranda's jive? That was your choreography?" Mary Ann asks.

"Put me down, please," Sophie says, but I pretend not to hear her. She sighs. "It was. It plays into Trevor's strengths with acrobatics and lifts. I think they did a terrific job. They've danced together for years, and Miranda's been my best friend since childhood. If I couldn't do it, there's no one else I'd rather have take my spot."

The girls share a hug, which is awkward because I'm holding Sophie, but it ends up being a group hug.

"I hate it was under these circumstances," Randi says once she pulls out of our hug. "But Trevor and I dreamed of appearing together on a show like this when we were in college, so it's exciting to cross it off the bucket list. I'm so grateful to the producers for the opportunity." She laughs self-deprecatingly. "No one cares about me. Let's talk about how wonderful a choreographer Sophie is! She's so creative. I'm in awe of her talent. I hope everyone votes so she has her chance to dance in the finale!"

The crowd cheers. Glen raises his hand to silence them.

"Ready for your scores?" he asks.

Before he raises his paddle, Glen smiles at Miranda. "If you decide you want to give this a go and be a pro, call me!"

Sophie keeps her smile firmly in place, but I can feel the tension Glen's statement causes in her. That he can so cavalierly offer it to Randi when Sophie has been working her ass off at it for years pisses me off. Even the sight of Glen holding up a ten doesn't make it better.

"That's yours," I whisper in her ear. When Carlo and Mary Ann also hold up tens, putting Randi and me at the top of the scoreboard, I press a kiss to her cheek before telling Ian, "They belong to your sister. We couldn't have done it without Sophie."

"She's awesome," Ian says. "The best choreographer I know."

We were the last couple to dance, so we only need to wait

through a commercial break and some chatter before the five couples stand on the dance floor and wait to be informed of our fates. Sophie is back in her seat in the audience next to Mac. I wanted to continue holding her in my arms for the results, but the director wouldn't let me, so I had to return her during the break. Something about three being a crowd. Asshole.

"How do you stand doing this each week?" Randi murmurs through her smile. "I feel like the prized poodle at a dog show."

"I thought you'd think of show ponies before dogs," I quip.

The cameraman counts us down as Ian and DeeDee prepare to give the results.

"Wow! We had an incredible audience vote tonight! Did America agree with our judges, or are we in for an upset?" DeeDee asks with wide-eyed anticipation.

"Only one way to find out, DeeDee." Ian waves a folded slip of paper. The paper's just for show—they get the results through their earpieces. "Are we ready?"

The crowd applauds on cue and quiets down after a few moments.

"As you know," Ian says, "only three couples will move on to next week's finals. You've all worked so hard and should be proud of yourselves, no matter your placement." That's not true though. The two couples that are announced safe are obviously feeling better than the three couples still on stage, knowing the odds are stacked against them being the couple to stay.

DeeDee makes a sad face for the camera. "The first couple we have to say goodbye to is..." I hold my breath, praying Sophie's dream isn't over. Randi and I both let out a whoosh and squeeze each other's hands when our names aren't called. We step to the center of the floor with the other remaining couple, wishing each other luck. They had a high score from the judges too, so it's not a slam dunk.

"It's time to find out who will dance in next week's finale," Ian says. "Good luck to both couples."

My eyes are locked with Sophie's as she sits clutching Mac's hand.

"The celebrity safe to dance in next week's final is…Trevor Carter!"

Randi squeals next to me and wraps me in a hug. Mac and Sophie are hugging, and she's wiping tears from her eyes.

On autopilot, we hug the departing couple and then back away so they can be the focus of the attention. I go to Sophie and pick her up in a hug. I want to kiss her in the worst way. Or the best way. Hell, I want to kiss Sophie Mackenzie in all the ways.

"We did it, princess," I say, laughing and spinning her around, mindful that I don't swing her injured ankle into anything.

"*You* did it, boyo. You and Miranda, thank you so much."

Randi joins our group hug, and so do Mac and Ian. I'm suddenly the filling of a Mackenzie sandwich, not something I ever expected to be.

A few hours later, the excitement has fizzled into frustration as I try to help Sophie through our hotel. We're staying overnight in New York before game two of our wild card series tomorrow night. Sophie's on crutches and refuses to let me carry her everywhere. Stubborn woman. Can't she see I need to take care of her? I need to make sure she doesn't injure herself further. And I want to take advantage of every moment I can to hold her in my arms. This time next week, our fling will be over. It's probably better to end it now before we get too attached and break our hearts. Okay, my heart is going to break, but if I can protect Sophie's, I will. Who knows? Maybe my worry is for nothing, and she hasn't changed her mind about wanting anything more than a fling.

Just because I'm dreading this ending doesn't mean she is. She's going to be living her dream as a pro on the show. She's going to have a new partner and work with him as closely as we did. Maybe they'll have a spark and he'll be the one she's meant to be with. She may not even be on the US version of the show. There are versions all over the world. She could end up on the UK show with Ian. Hell, she could end up in Australia or New Zealand. She won't want to be tied down when all of that's available to her.

Putting down our dance bags, I grab water bottles from the mini fridge and offer one to Sophie after she's settled on the sofa.

"You need to elevate your foot, honey. Do you want it on the table or on the sofa?" I bend down to press a quick kiss to her lips. "Lap?" I sit next to her on the sofa, and she rests her bandaged ankle on the throw pillow I place on my lap. "How's it feeling?"

Sophie wiggles her toes. "Throbby. But I should be okay to dance on Sunday or Monday. I've had worse. It's just damn inconvenient timing. The final is a freestyle dance of our choice. We can do whatever we want. It doesn't have to be ballroom or Latin. It can be contemporary, tap, ballet."

"Hmm..." I rest my hands on her uninjured leg. "Do you have any ideas? Do you like dancing contemporary? I've had ballet training."

She cocks her head, making her blonde ponytail swing to the side. It's irresistible, like golden silk running through my fingers.

"You had ballet training? Really?"

"Yeah, until I was thirteen. That's when I got more involved with hockey and stopped taking dance lessons with my cousins. I enjoyed it when I got to partner with girls who weren't my cousins." I chuckle. "I was bigger and stronger than most boys my age, so I'd often pair the older girls who were more developed than girls my age. Just as well I stopped. Things were getting embarrassing as I hit puberty. Tights don't hide a damn thing, you know."

Her tinkling laugh makes my heart happy. "Yeah, with all you've been blessed with, there's no hiding it."

That earns her a kiss on the tip of her nose. "Thank you for noticing."

"Well, it's kinda hard to miss!"

"Kinda hard is always accurate when I'm with you."

She pouts. "Just kinda? We need to fix that."

Leaning forward, she lifts her sweater over her head, leaving her in a pale blue lace bra that lovingly cups her breasts.

I reach out to trace a fingertip along the edge of her bra. Goose-bumps pebble her skin. Not from a chill, more from the heat between us.

"How do you propose we do that?" I ask. I know what I'd like to do, but she's the one with the injury we need to be mindful of.

"Hmm..." Sophie cups her chin in a classic thinking pose. "I need to keep my ankle elevated, so if I keep it thrown over your shoulder, that should do the trick. I've heard that endorphins are natural painkillers, and orgasms release endorphins. Do you have any aches that need relief?"

It's my turn to adopt a thinking pose. I tap a fingertip against my lip, scrunch my face a bit, and look toward the ceiling. Sophie's thinking face is much cuter. Hell, everything about Sophie is cuter.

"I think I have a few. Probably best if we move to the bed, so we have room to relieve them."

Her grin is mischievous. "I fit on this sofa just fine. What's the problem?"

My hand slides up the leg of her black slacks, seeking the spot behind her knee that I know is ticklish.

"Don't you dare," she warns. "Not unless you want something to ache for a whole other reason."

My fingers tiptoe back down her calf, away from the danger zone. She has brothers. I know this isn't an idle threat. I scoop her up in my arms and stand. The room isn't big, so it only takes a couple of steps to get to the king-size bed. Mindful of Sophie's injury, I place her gently on the bed and straighten so I can remove my shirt. She's reaching behind to unclasp her bra and then reaching to open the closure of her slacks.

I cover her hands with mine. "Lay back, I'll take care of it. I'll take care of everything." My wink is flirty. "Enjoy your endorphins."

We work together to slide her pants down her legs without putting any stress on her injured ankle. The lacy blue panties that match her bra are all she's wearing. I remove them with my teeth after kissing my way up her uninjured leg. Knowing how important it is for Sophie to keep her ankle elevated, I don't take any chances and place both legs over my shoulders. Safety first.

The scent of her arousal is intoxicating. The taste of her is ambrosia. I'd be happy to do this for the rest of my life. Forget hockey, forget dance, just let me be in this bed with Sophie. Let the outside world forget we exist.

But that's not possible. So we'll have to take what we can from the moments we have left. I take my time nuzzling along the inside of Sophie's slender thighs, dropping teasing kisses and little nips as I get ever closer to her core. The strong muscles of her legs tremble from desire. Her ankle rubs against my back when I finally apply my tongue and fingers where her whimpers and pleas have been begging me to be. When she's trembling from the aftershocks of her first orgasm, I give one last languid lick, grab a condom from the hotel nightstand, and make quick work of sheathing myself. Thank goodness Sophie is a goddess of flexibility so we can keep her ankle elevated as I slowly push in her.

We both sigh at the rightness of being together. I force myself to remain in the moment and not think about how this will be one of the last times we're together like this. All that matters is now, and I'm going to give her every last part of me because after loving Sophie, I'll never love anyone like this again. With every stroke and caress, I let my body tell her what I can't say with words. When we've both reached our release and are cuddling under the covers, I want to weep. For the first time, I'm thinking about giving up on my vow not to have kids. I like kids; I love my nephews. It's not that I think I'll be a bad father; I'd make sure everyone had what they needed. But I know I'd be doing it to make Sophie happy, and I'm afraid I'd resent it. I can't do that to her or to our children. I won't ever let someone I love feel like they weren't the life I dreamed of.

20

SOPHIE

THEY LOST. AGAIN. THE DEVIL BIRDS NEED TO WIN THE REMAINING THREE games of this wild card round to remain in the hunt for the Dickinson Cup. The next two games will be back in Atlantic City, so they'll have home-ice advantage. Trevor hasn't said anything aloud, but I can tell by his slumped shoulders when he thinks no one's looking that he thinks their season is doomed. Even with a hockey-playing brother, I never knew how superstitious hockey players are with their rituals and lucky socks and stuff. Trevor's mumbling about how things he's done all season long are no longer working.

He's started talking in his sleep about how maybe they've been right all along and he doesn't belong on the team. That he's not good enough and only on the team because of nepotism and the rest of the team has carried him all season long. It breaks my heart to hear him say those things, for him only to feel vulnerable enough to share it when he's asleep and unaware. There's nothing I can do for him to make it better other than hold him and whisper back that he's good enough, he deserves to be there, he's an important part of the team's success. I hope my words sink into his subconscious and quiet the nastiness his mind conjures up when he's not strong enough to fight back.

Five more days. That's all I have with Trevor. We've started to learn the choreography of our dance for the finals tomorrow. It's been two days since my injury during dress rehearsal. My ankle is healed, and I'm cleared to dance. Bless shifter healing. I'm taking Trevor's strengths—literally and artistically—into account while planning the choreography, including lots of lifts, which will help me not put too much stress on my ankle. Even though it's healed, I know the risks of reinjury if I put too much strain on it too soon.

We're alone in the barn's dance studio. We do our taped rehearsals with Nigel at Devil's Den but having private time to dance, just the two of us, without having to filter anything, is freeing.

"Argh!" Trevor yells, pulling at his hair in frustration because he missed a step.

"Hey," I murmur, wrapping my arms around his waist and pressing a kiss to his pec. "It's okay."

His eyes are closed as he presses a kiss to my forehead.

"Are you okay?" I ask. Obviously he's not, but I don't know if it's because of dance or hockey or us.

"Five days," he says.

My breath catches. "What?"

"Five days until the finale. Of the show." In a softer voice, he adds, "Of us."

I swallow past the lump in my throat. "That's what we agreed to. It's the right thing to do. To drag it on would only hurt you." There's no holding back the sadness in my voice.

"Hurt me? What do you mean?" His brows draw together as he looks down at me. I step out of his arms and start to pace. If he's holding me while I tell him the truth, it will break me when he lets me go.

He holds out his hand, and in a moment of weakness, I place mine in his. He gives it a gentle squeeze. "What do you mean about hurting me?"

I pull my hand from his, my shoulders hunched under the weight of what I need to tell him.

"Soph?"

"We agreed it was just going to be for the run of the show. A fling," I say.

"We did," he says evenly.

"I don't want to hurt you, Trevor. I can't give you what you want." I swallow heavily, trying to keep my sobs from bubbling up.

"What is it you think I want?"

I let out a shuddering breath. "Marriage, kids, a wife at home. I can't do that, Trevor. I can't be that woman. I don't think I ever want children. I'm selfish. I want my career. My mother sacrificed years of dancing to raise us. My father's horses and their races were more important than dance competitions. She trained me and Ian, and that's when she started performing again. But that's just because she was there for us. We were still the focus. It wasn't until we were all grown that she joined the show." She shakes her head. "I can't do that. I *won't* do that. No matter how much I love you."

My hands fly to my mouth, and I can feel my eyes widen in shock. Crap. I didn't mean to say that last part. I do love him. But I didn't mean to say it out loud.

I must have shocked Trevor too. That is the only reason that damn man should be laughing at a time like this. At least I don't have to worry about tears anymore—the way my blood is starting to boil is evaporating them.

"Thrilled you find this so amusing, Trevor. Forget I said anything." I turn and walk over to my phone to restart the song. We may as well get back to dancing. That's all that matters now.

"No," he says, jumping in front of me and grabbing my hands. He raises them to his lips and kisses the backs of them gently.

"My darling Sophie. I'm laughing because you are so incredibly wrong. I don't want kids anytime soon, if ever. I want to focus on my hockey career and be free to travel. I don't want to be tied down.

Metaphorically. Literally, could be fun sometime. Our safe word would be pineapple."

That gets a laugh out of me.

"Seriously. I grew up as an afterthought. I was a mistake. My parents love me, but I messed up their plans. They took care of me physically and materially, but emotionally, they were past the little kid stage. They were happy to have my aunts and uncles care for me. Put me in whatever activity would keep me busy and out of their hair. I won't ever do that to a child. I like kids, but I don't want to give up what I enjoy for them. One of the things I really like about kids is the ability to give them back. I don't know if my opinion will ever change. I know how it is for wolf shifters. We're supposed to want kids and a pack. Especially female wolf shifters. You come from a large family. I assumed that's what you'd want."

I blink up at him. I can't believe what I'm hearing. "You don't want to get married and have kids?"

He shakes his head. "Not anytime soon. Maybe not ever. That's why I wanted a fling. I didn't want to lead you on and have you expecting me to propose or want kids." He leads me over to the chairs in the corner of the studio and kneels in front of me. I open my legs to accommodate him scooting closer.

"Sophie, I love you too. These past couple of months with you have been wonderful. I don't want to stop seeing you. I know we both have our careers, and that means we won't have a traditional relationship, but I don't want to be with anyone else. We're together whenever we can be. I can come to you when the hockey season is over. What do you think?"

"Yes, absolutely yes!" I exclaim, wrapping my arms around him before kissing him passionately. I could do this forever. I want to do this forever.

But we have five days until the finale. We need to focus.

Reluctantly, I pull back from our kiss. "Now that we have that settled, we can spend the next five days getting this dance perfect. Okay?"

He sighs but nods. "Okay, but after the five days, no more using dance as an excuse to put off talking about our future." The wink he gives lets me know he's teasing.

"What is it with your family and this song?" Trevor asks as we take our opening positions. We're dancing to a slowed-down version of "(I'm Gonna Be) 500 Miles" by The Proclaimers. We've gone over the moves by counts and now we need to start doing it to music.

My brow furrows as I look up at him. "What?"

"Mac and Randi sang a duet version on New Year's Eve."

My heart melts hearing that. I wish I'd been there early enough to see it. "Really? That's so cool! You know The Proclaimers are Scottish, right?"

He nods.

"It's our father's favorite song and what he'd sing to us when it was his turn to put us to bed. You've heard him, he has a deep, rumbly burr. My earliest memory is being held by him with my cheek resting on his chest as he sang and feeling it vibrate through me. I felt so safe and loved. I don't know if my brothers felt the same way, but Dec is the most sentimental of us, so I could see him liking it for similar reasons."

He nods, looking thoughtful. I wonder if knowing the personal connection I have to the song makes a difference. We start in opposite corners of the dance floor and jog toward each other, clasping hands as we pass and turning to face one another. He pulls me toward him and swings me into an inverted lift before gently lowering me back to my feet. The whole routine is a lot of pushing and pulling, pretty reminiscent of our relationship. But we always come back together even after we're apart. We do a lot of lifts, but they aren't the acrobatic and cheer lifts we've done previously—these are more ballet than football field. We don't even discuss the moves—we do them instinctually, knowing what's right for the music and for each other. It's as if admitting our feelings for each other has torn down the wall between us and made dancing together effortless. I've never danced from the heart the way I am with this dance. To save my ankle, we do a lot of turns on my other foot and any landings are done softly. I know I'm technically healed, but I don't want anything to jeopardize being able to dance on tour this summer.

Our ending pose is with us sitting side by side, facing each other. Trevor pulls me into his lap and kisses the daylight out of me. That's not how we're going to do it in the ballroom, but for today, for us, it's the perfect ending. Or beginning. Whatever it is, it's perfection.

21

SOPHIE

"You're like a good luck charm!" Teagan says, laughing and hugging those of us in the owners' box at the fourth wild card game. The Devil Birds won it, tying the series and forcing a game five in New York to decide who advances to the first round of the Dickinson Cup playoffs. Trevor broke his slump and scored hat tricks in both games, a first-time accomplishment in the PHL. He's earned a place in the league's history. No one can claim he doesn't deserve his spot on the team now.

Laughing, I return her hug. "It's all Trevor. He's been working so hard. I'm thrilled for him and for the team!"

We're a joyous group as we make our way down to the locker room area. I can't wait to see Trevor and congratulate him. I know they have one more game to play in this round, but it really feels like they have momentum on their side. Players are being interviewed in the hallway, so we watch. Trevor's talking to someone from the national broadcast.

"Great game, Trevor. Hat tricks in back-to-back games. That's extremely rare. What do you attribute this sudden scoring burst to?"

the extremely perky redhead asks as she thrusts her microphone in his face.

"Thanks, Hayley. Everything is coming together at just the right time. We're a cohesive team. The hat tricks may be attributed to me, but they wouldn't have happened without my teammates." He sees me standing down the hallway and gives me a wink. Miranda gives a happy squeak and squeezes my arm. She loves that two of her best friends are in love with each other. Honestly, she's in love with love. She wants everyone to pair up and be as happy as she is with Declan.

"Back to New York for game five Thursday night. Shame you won't compete in the finals for *Celebrity Dance Dare*. You were favored to win." Hayley's statement rips a gasp from me. I didn't realize game five was scheduled on the same night as the finale. Judging from Trevor's stunned expression, he didn't either.

"I wasn't aware of the schedule. Is that official?" He's looking around for someone, but I don't know who. He's not looking at me, which is good. I'm able to slip away from the group before the tears fall. We've spent the past few days perfecting a beautiful routine to "500 Miles" no one will ever see.

Daphne slips her arm through mine. "Let's go to my office. It's right down the hall."

I gratefully accept the bottle of water and box of tissues she offers.

"I'm going back because there's stuff I need to deal with. I'll let Trevor know you're here, okay?" I nod as she slips out the door.

The click of the door closing is like a switch, turning on the tears. I was so close to doing it. I was going to prove I belonged as a pro. That I was as good as Ian and didn't need my spot as a favor. I deserved it because I was the best. Now I'll be an asterisk on the show's Wikipedia page as a finalist who didn't compete. I'll still be Ian's sister, not a Platinum Paw winner. There's no question Trevor's going to choose to play in game five instead of dancing. That's what he should do. He's worked so hard to get here, and his team needs him. I want him to have this.

I'm not sure how long I sit there, trying to control myself, when Miranda pokes her head in.

"Hey, Soph. Can you come with me?" she asks.

"Yeah." I shove some tissues in the pocket of the hoodie I'm wearing with Trevor's name and number on the back.

We take the elevator to the floor where the administrative offices are. There's carpeting instead of cement floors, and it doesn't smell of sweaty hockey gear. She raps on the door with Jake Whitman's name on it. He's the general manager and third co-owner of the Devil Birds. I don't know him as well as I've gotten to know Teagan and Liam, the rest of the team's ownership. Trevor opens the door, grabs my hand, and pulls me into a hug.

"Sophie, I'm so sorry. We're trying to work this out." He's murmuring next to my ear and holding me tightly. I think it's to comfort me, but maybe he needs comfort too.

His team T-shirt is soft as I wrap my arms around his back. It's slightly damp, like he threw it on the moment he got out of the shower and rushed to be here.

"It's okay," I whisper.

Jake is pacing behind his desk, talking into his phone to I don't know who. "You make us put a player on the reality TV show. He does a great job and brings lots of attention to the PHL. And you're going to punish him and his partner for their success by making him choose between being there for his team or fulfilling his obligation to his partner and the show *you made him do*? What the fuck is this? Adjust the damn schedule. Make game five a day later."

"We can't do that!" The voice on the other end of the call is so loud, I hear him like he's standing in the room with us. "That's not how it's done!"

"That's Barry Wagerman," Trevor whispers in my ear. "Interim league commissioner."

"Bullshit!" Jake yells. "It's the first year of playoffs. You can do whatever you want. Tickets haven't even gone on sale yet! Unless there's a reason you want to hinder our chances of advancing to the next round. I've spoken to New York's manager, and they have no objection to playing the next day. They'd love an extra break day. You can ask them yourself." Jake shoves his fingers through his dark hair and then tugs it in frustration. "The whole point of having Carter on the show was to get people watching our games. It's idiotic to make the new fans we've gained from *Celebrity Dance Dare* choose between watching the game or the finale. If you make them choose, they aren't choosing the game."

"We can't move the game," Wagerman says. "Our broadcast partners want the game on Thursday, and we have to honor their wishes."

"That's ridiculous!" Teagan bursts into the room and walks over to Jake's side. "It's the end of February. There could be a blizzard causing the game to be postponed and the schedule would be adjusted. That just happened in Buffalo! Games that have been scheduled for months get postponed and moved. Certainly a game that just became a necessity and doesn't have tickets sold for it yet can be moved a day in either direction."

"Ms. Penhall, my hands are tied. The game's on Thursday evening. Your player is either on the ice or not. That's a team matter, not a league matter. Discussion closed." Wagerman disconnects the call.

Teagan pulls out her phone and types quickly.

Jake reads over her shoulder and snorts. "Teag, you can't ask your parents to buy a television network just because you're pissed off. It may not even be the network's issue. This could be Wagerman trying to wave his tiny dick around."

Jake flushes and apologizes when he realizes what he said in mixed company. Like I care. I've heard worse. Hell, I've *said* worse.

"Sophie," Jake says, "we're reaching out to CDD production to see what our options are. Maybe you guys can be judged on a recorded performance, or they can be flexible with the broadcast?"

"Maybe." But I know the answer is going to be no. I'm just not ready to admit it out loud. "I'm going to New York tomorrow to rehearse for the finals. I have group dances to learn. No matter what happens with the hockey game, I'm contractually obligated to be at the finale."

"We're going to work this out, Soph," Trevor tells me. I can see the sincerity shining in his eyes and love him for it. But it won't work out. It never works out. I've accepted it.

I grab a fistful of his T-shirt so I can pull his lips down to mine and give him a too-quick kiss. "It's okay. Follow what the league says." I lower my voice. "This is your dream. Go along with what they say, don't make waves. This is your career, and it's impacting the entire team. It's not worth making a ruckus."

Trevor growls in frustration. "Sophie, your career matters too!"

Mindful of the others in the room, I murmur, "Let's talk about this at home."

Home. We've made that little pool house our home without realizing it. No matter what else is happening, that's our safe haven. He nods.

"Do you need us for anything, Jake?" Trevor asks.

"No, we're okay. Sophie, I promise we're going to do everything we can to work this out. It's not right for you to be impacted by the league's stupidity." Jake sighs and shakes his head. "You've both worked so hard and deserve to be rewarded for it. I'm sorry. If I knew this was a possibility, I'd have told the league to shove doing the show up their ass."

He's such a nice man. "Thanks, Jake. It's okay. It's just a dance. The show will go on, regardless."

That's what I tell myself. It's just a dance. One dance. I've proven what I can do all season long. I'm either good enough or not. And if I'm not? Well, I'll have to accept that. Even if I knew this was how this was going to end, I wouldn't have traded this opportunity to dance with Trevor and fall in love with him. I wish I could cast a spell that would make Trevor being in two places at once possible. Unfortunately, not even Teagan is a powerful enough witch to make that happen.

We're quiet on the drive home. I'm not mad at Trevor. I'm not mad at anyone. There's no point. In the pool house, I run an Epsom salt bath for Trevor to soak in. It was a very physical game, and Trevor was involved in some massive hits—giving and receiving—and it'll help relieve the aches and pains. I climb in with him because it soothes my ankle, and being near him soothes my heart.

Now that we don't have a deadline on our relationship, the desperation to make love—because that's what we've been doing—isn't as strong. We still want each other, of course, but we know we have time. It's not now or never.

Later, I'm the little spoon to Trevor's big spoon in our bed.

"Trevor, it's okay," I say into the darkness. I know this is weighing heavily on him, and I hate that. He should revel in being the team hero these past two games. He should be looking forward to winning this series and then rolling through the Dickinson Cup playoffs. They can win the whole thing. Trevor deserves this. He didn't ask to do *Celebrity Dance Dare*. He was told he had to do it and was a good enough sport to go along with it and try his best. He doesn't owe me or the show anything.

Trevor drives me to the airport in the early morning. I'm traveling to New York with Jake, who's on a mission to make this work out so Trevor can do both events. Trevor will ride with the team on the bus later this morning. We're in separate hotels tonight, but tomorrow night we'll be together again. It'll be weird to not sleep in his arms, but I'll have to get used to it. We each have busy lives with lots of travel. I spend our flight with my head resting against the helicopter window, listening to Jake type away on his laptop. The rhythm makes me think of tap dancing, and an idea for a routine develops.

It's weird to be at the dance studio without Trevor at my side. The wardrobe folks insist on having final dance outfits ready for me and Trevor because "miracles happen." I don't know what fantasyland they live in, but in my world, there's no point hoping for miracles because there's only disappointment when you don't get them. Being around the crew of the show as just a dancer in the troupe is strangely comforting. I don't need to worry about Trevor being okay, not letting nerves get to him. This is what I love about the show. The buzz backstage, talking to the other dancers, not having my attention divided. Of course, I loved dancing with Trevor, but I think it's mainly because it was with Trevor.

"Hey, twinster," Ian says, joining me in the wardrobe room. "Are you okay?"

Shrugging, I sigh. There's no point in saying anything. Ian knows what I'm thinking.

"You guys have a dance, right? It's all choreographed?"

"Of course. Oh, Ian, it's beautiful. Do you wanna see?"

At his nod, I grab my phone and scroll to the video we shot. It's not a perfect recording, but good enough. The song ends, and Ian just stares at the screen.

"Wow," my brother says. "That's the best thing you've ever choreographed. It's beautiful. It needs to be seen."

Shrugging, I put my phone away. "We'll see what happens. It's enough that it exists."

"Bullshit!" He stomps away, only to turn around and stalk back to me. "And stop being so Zen. It's creepy."

I huff out a laugh. Being creepy is the least of my issues.

Ian fists his hands on his hips. "You're dancing that dance on the finale. If Trevor isn't here, I'll dance it with you. They'll be short a number and have already cleared the music, so the producers won't have a problem." He wraps his arm around my shoulders. "The two of you are wonderful together."

"Yeah, he's an excellent dancer."

He chuckles. "I don't mean as a dance team. I mean, as a couple, you're right for each other. I'm glad you found that."

"How do you know? You only see us one day a week."

"I talk to Declan. By the way, we need to start the betting pools on when he and Miranda get engaged, when the wedding will be, and how long before we have a little niece or nephew."

"Declan likes us together?" He never said he didn't, but I didn't know if that was approval or minding his own business.

"Very much. He respects Trevor and appreciates how he treats you."

Tears fill my eyes. I like that my brothers approve. I lean forward and wrap Ian in a fierce hug.

"I'm so glad you're here, Ian," I whisper past my tight throat. I can't imagine having to go through today alone.

He hugs me back, presses a kiss to my hair. "Even though I'm horning in on your show? I'm sorry, Sophie. I didn't think about how you'd feel with me showing up. This was your chance to be in the spotlight, and I think I hogged some of it. I'm a selfish clod sometimes. I didn't think about how advancing my career was going to make yours harder."

I pull back, nodding. We need to have this conversation. This probably isn't the best day to have it, but I may as well shove all the suckiness together rather than letting it ruin multiple days.

"I love you, Ian. I'm so proud of you. But for once, I wanted to be the Mackenzie in the spotlight. Everyone knows the only reason I have my spot on the show is because you and Ma required it."

"What?" Ian's brow is furrowed. He looks truly puzzled.

"Your contract included a clause that I'd be included in the troupe for the UK show and given a spot in this show."

Ian shakes his head slowly. "No, it doesn't. Neither does Ma's. Neither one of us has that kind of influence. Who told you that?"

"Nancy. And other people have whispered that I only have this shot because of you both."

He somehow manages to snort elegantly. If I tried that I'd sound like an asthmatic alpaca.

"Never, ever listen to anything that bitch says. She's a bitter, petty woman. Of course being related to us helped you get noticed, but that's because we were dance partners for years. They saw you when they were watching my tapes. It got my other former partners noticed too. None of them made the show because they aren't as good as you. The only thing they had going for them was being half a foot taller than you. I used to pray every night you'd have a growth spurt so we could keep dancing together. Told you I was selfish."

He reaches out and presses against my chin to close my mouth. I didn't realize it had fallen open in shock.

"So you had nothing to do with me being on the show?" Could this be true? Could I have gotten this on my own merits?

"It's true. I had nothing to do with you getting a spot. Other than being an excellent partner when we were younger. You got yourself here, crumpet. Why do you listen to idiots? You know how catty dancers are."

I listen to idiots because they confirm what I believe about myself. I'm not ready to admit that out loud yet. Ian's knowing gaze tells me I don't have to. He can see the truth. Having a twin who knows me so well is a blessing and a curse.

I pull him in for another hug and kiss him on the cheek. "I'm so glad you're here, Ian. Seriously. You're wonderful as a host, and if I can't dance with Trevor, there's no one else I'd rather dance with. Thank you."

He gives my ponytail a light tug. "Stop being so sappy, Soph. It's almost as creepy as you being Zen. Let's go remind everyone what a great team we make."

The day is a blur of learning and rehearsing the group dances for the finale. While the other two teams rehearse their final dances, I teach Ian ours. He learns all the steps quickly and is technically perfect, but I know the dance is missing the magic that occurs when it's me and Trevor performing. The league wouldn't relent on rescheduling the game, so Trevor and I aren't competing for the Platinum Paw. Ian and I will dance it as an exhibition dance instead.

Ma swings by and is given the star treatment by the producers in deference to her role as a judge on the main UK show. And because she's wonderful. She's not interested in all that though. Today she just wants to be my mum, and I love her for it. For the first time since the debacle with Doreen, I have a cup of tea. I'm only drinking it because it's my mother's special blend, and it has always calmed me down. We're settled on a settee in the green room, which is deserted for once. It's wonderful to be my mother's focus. It's been too long since it's been just the two of us.

"Sophie girl, I am so proud of you," Ma says in her soothing Irish lilt. "You've worked so hard and come so far. And to see you with Trevor, ach, it does my heart good. All I want is to see my children happy, to see them find the love they deserve. I wish you much happiness together. Like what I have with your father."

I need to tell her the truth, but I'm afraid. Now that I have her approval, I don't want to lose it. But I'm tired of hiding a part of myself.

"Ma, I don't want what you and Da have. I don't want to be tied down with kids. I don't want to give up dancing. I love Trevor, but I don't know that I want to marry him. Or if he'd want to marry me. He doesn't want kids either. You had to give up dancing when you had us, and Da's horses and races always came first. I'm selfish. I want to put myself first."

The hurt in her blue eyes kills me. I love my mother. Even though her choices aren't what I want for myself, I don't want to belittle her for making them. She loves us, and I'm grateful to have her as my mother.

"Is that what you think?" Ma asks.

Swallowing hard, I nod.

Tears gather in Ma's eyes as she takes my hand. "Oh, Sophie, I'm sorry. I failed you."

My shocked gasp seems to echo off the walls and slam back into me. That was not what I was expecting.

"I never wanted it to seem like I gave up anything to raise you and your brothers. I didn't. I wanted to be a wife and mother. I didn't plan to have so many of you so quickly"—she grins and shrugs— "but it is what it is. I'd always wanted to have a family. But that's what was right for me. You don't have to want the same thing."

"But you had to stop dancing. I know you love it."

Ma shakes her head. "I never gave up dancing. I gave up competing. Two different things. I never enjoyed competing, but it's what you endure to be able to dance ballroom at the level I wanted. By the time I married your father, I'd accomplished what I wanted in the professional ballroom world. I'd won the championships, done the travel. I was ready for a new adventure. You and your brothers were certainly that!"

We both laugh.

"But I always kept dancing," she says. "I'd dance with you in my arms while you were infants. Your father's thing was to sing to you, mine was to dance. I taught you and your brothers to dance. Your father and I would dance. I dance amongst the flowers in my garden. I'm never going to stop dancing. What I gave up was the hours of practicing. The weeks of travel. The strict dieting. You're blessed with a shifter metabolism, so staying trim and strong is easy for you. For those of us who are all human, even with my powers as a witch, it's a struggle. I had to exercise strenuously and be mindful of every calorie to stay in the shape required to dance competitively at the highest levels. No way could I enjoy the delicious treats Siobhan made. No tea parties with you and Miranda. Competing wasn't worth the sacrifice. If I'd wanted to keep competing, your father would have supported me wholeheartedly, just as he does with the show. All he's ever done is love and support me."

A tear slips down my cheek as I nod. I didn't know any of this.

"You were all babies, so you have no way of knowing, but Seamus was a difficult pregnancy. To have more children would've been dangerous for me. We wanted a large family, but two sets of twins back-to-back, and then to be surprised with Seamus... My body never had a chance to recover. Your father went and got the snip to protect me. You know men, and you know wolf shifters. They're a virile lot, and their manhood is everything. But your father went and did that for me, for us, without a second thought. I didn't even ask him, he did it. So, aye, let him have his horses and his races, they make him happy. But I know his heart lies with me and our family."

"I...I never knew any of this," I stammer. "All I saw was you sacrificing. I know I'm too selfish to do that."

"Sophie, you are not selfish. It's okay to not want to be a wife and mother. I know the wolves are an old-fashioned lot, but we live in the modern world. Women, even women who are wolf shifters, are entitled to live the lives they want. Whether that's focusing on a career, or focusing around hearth and home, or melding both. You can be whoever you want and do what is best for you. I'm going to love and support you no matter what. I am so proud of you. Whether you dance or change diapers or dig for dinosaur bones, whatever you want to do, I want for you. Your job is to live the life that pleases you, not what you think pleases me. I made my choices. You get to make yours."

I don't know if this counts as a conversation since I barely said anything, but it's the conversation I needed to have. The sobs come unexpectedly as Ma pulls me into her embrace. I'm shedding tears of relief at admitting the truth of how I feel, sorrow for the years I spent resenting the choices my mother made and the expectations I felt they placed on me, and also tears of joy knowing I'm accepted for who I am. I don't have to fit into a mold to be loved. Part of me wishes I'd done this sooner, but I know now is when I needed to hear it the most.

My mom got to live her dreams. So did Dad. And that really fills me with joy.

But the next second, it comes crashing down because from where I'm sitting, neither Trevor nor I get to live ours.

22

TREVOR

I'VE FAILED. EVERYTHING I'VE TRIED TO BOTH BE ABLE TO PERFORM ON THE *Celebrity Dance Dare* finale and play in the final game of this series has been met with failure. The PHL refuses to start the game an hour later so I could perform our finale dance first and then race the few blocks back to the arena to suit up in time for puck drop. I wouldn't even stay for scores. I'd perform and dash. No-go. They insist on puck drop going off right on time, and if I'm not there, I'm not playing. I'm not even allowed to leave and come back. I'll be guarded like a prisoner once the game starts. If I leave the arena, they won't let me back in, and the Devil Birds can't substitute a player. They'd have to play a man down the rest of the game.

Jake and Teagan argued everything they could. Even the coach and manager of the New York team tried to get Wagerman to see reason, to no avail. I'm only a few blocks away from Sophie and the dance studio, but it may as well be a million miles. We've texted and had a brief video chat today when she had snippets of time available. She's going to dance our dance with Ian. I'm glad it's going to be seen—it deserves to be seen. I just wish it was me dancing it with her.

"Dude, can you stare vacantly into space in another direction, you're freaking me out," Stone says from his space across the locker room from me. That's when I realize I've been staring at him as he's putting on the base layer of his uniform. We've all seen each other naked. It's not a big deal, but I can see how it would be unnerving.

"Sorry," I mumble, averting my gaze to the floor. I should be putting on my own gear and getting ready to hit the ice, but for the first time ever, there's no thrill of excitement at hearing the crowd and anticipating the feel of my blades slicing through the fresh ice.

I don't want to do this. I don't want to be here. I should be with Sophie. I *want* to be with Sophie. It's not about winning the competition. I don't give a fuck if *I* win, but I want her to win. I don't have to prove to anyone I'm a good hockey player. I think my two hat tricks this week speak for themselves. I care about my teammates, of course. I don't want to let them down, but they don't need me. They've proven they can win without me on the ice. Sophie needs me. Just as importantly, I need Sophie.

I stand, about to find Coach, only to discover him standing there with Jake, watching me.

"Go," Coach says. "We got your back. You've had ours all season."

I check my watch. I have fifteen minutes to get to the studio. I need to change. I can't dance in the suit I wore to arrive at the game. Jake tosses me a T-shirt and a pair of joggers.

"Randi says to wear this and to haul your ass there. She's texted Ian."

I'm changed and out the door in minutes, leaving a flurry of break-a-legs and go-get-ems in my wake. I can't trust a taxi, so I run like a crazy person the few blocks to the studio where the show is filming. Thank the stars the security staff recognizes me and lets me in without a fuss. Xavier grabs me and pulls me into the makeup room. Ian let him in on our plan.

"Relax," X says, "you have time. Let's get you ready. Catch your breath. Need to have you looking your best when you go out there and steal America's heart."

I submit to his handiwork and watch the feed of the show from the makeup chair. I keep checking the game's score on my phone. Scoreless in the first period and halfway through the second. Both teams are playing hard, desperate for the W. I know I made the right decision. This is where I need to be, this is where I want to be. I never expected to want to be somewhere other than on the ice during such a vital game, but I can't imagine being anywhere else. Sophie needs me, and nothing will stop me from being here for her. I don't need to prove to anyone that I'm good enough. Sophie Mackenzie loves me, and that's all that matters. I don't need the world when I have my girl.

23
SOPHIE

RUSHING BACKSTAGE AFTER PERFORMING A NUMBER WITH THE OTHER PROS and troupe dancers, I think about how easy it was to slip out of the laser focus I've always had with dance and connect with Trevor. Any other finale day, even when I was just a background dancer, my focus was completely on the performance ahead. If you weren't on the floor with me, you didn't exist. I'm still focused on dancing, but it exists along with other parts of life. Is this what it's like to have balance? I've never had that before. It's kinda nice.

I choreographed the pro dance, and it went well. It was relaxing not to have to explain every step and gesture because the pros understood what I was doing. I'm not as patient a teacher as Ian is. After two or three times, I want it to be perfect and move on to the next thing. But I hate moving on before it's perfect, so multiple repeats are necessary. It's frustrating, and I suck at hiding that. Thank goodness Trevor is easygoing and loves me.

Ian and I are dancing last. The two couples still competing for the Platinum Paw trophy danced well. Watching their dances, I sincerely think Trevor and I could've won with our choreography, but it doesn't matter. Nothing was announced about Trevor not dancing tonight. I assume DeeDee will say something for the television broadcast, and maybe the studio announcer will say something for the ballroom. Whatever. It doesn't really matter why he's not here.

When it's time for my freestyle dance, I go to my mark in the far corner of the dance floor and face the audience. I can feel everyone's eyes on me. It's my time in the spotlight. I thought I'd be excited. I am. But I'm also eerily calm. It doesn't matter how this dance goes because I'm not dancing it with Trevor. It's just steps and music, not our hearts and our feelings for each other. It's hollow. My parents and brothers—minus Declan—are here to support me. Mom insisted she was just a proud mother and didn't want to be introduced or acknowledged. It's my night. Mom makes heart hands, and my brothers are smiling. Dad's eyes are glassy. Okay, can't look at Dad, he'll make me cry. Someone yells out, "I love you, Sophie Macken-zie!" but it wasn't Trevor's voice, just a random fan.

The first notes of the music play. Ian's going to enter from the upper opposite corner so he's not visible to the audience yet. We're dancing to a dreamy arrangement of The Proclaimers' "(I'm Gonna Be) 500 Miles." The choreography includes more ballet and lifts than Ian and I are used to doing together. It suits Trevor's style of dance well and minimizes the stress on my ankle. I count, and I know when Ian enters the dance floor because I hear the audience react.

I turn and prepare to run toward Ian as the choreography calls for.

But I stop. It's not Ian.

It's Trevor. He's here. On the dance floor. To dance with me. He walks toward me with his hand outstretched. I take it, automatically.

"What are you doing?" I ask.

"Dancing with the woman I love," he says. He gives me a patented Trevor Carter flirty wink. "Let's do this."

My brain stops thinking, and I follow my heart as Trevor and I dance. I feel like I'm floating. Our lifts are effortless, the music flows. We're dancing in a snow globe. It's magical. The final pose has us sitting side by side, facing each other, with my hand resting on

Trevor's cheek. I don't stop there. I lean forward and kiss him with all the love in my heart as the last notes fade. We keep kissing even as the audience bursts into applause. It's only my father's very loud, very stern "ahem" that breaks through and has us separating.

Trevor pulls me to my feet and leads me over to Ian, who's wiping his eyes. The judges are passing a box of tissues down the line. My parents are hugging, and Mom is wiping Dad's eyes.

"I don't understand," I say. "Why aren't you at the game?"

"We couldn't work it out for me to do both, so I'm here. I couldn't let you down. I'm just part of the Devil Birds team. There are other people who can do what I do. You come first with me, Sophie. Always. I love you."

Ian holds out the box of tissues for me, and I grab a bunch. I can't speak, so I just nestle against Trevor's chest. He's wearing the black Devil Birds T-shirt with Shifty the Seagull on the front and jogger-style dance pants the wardrobe people got ready for him. They knew. They planned this. He's barefoot. He looks like he does at home when we're watching TV, and I love him for it.

"Ready to hear from the judges?" Ian asks after coughing to clear his throat. He has his hand resting on Trevor's shoulder in a brotherly fashion.

"We're being judged?" I ask, realizing that duh, we're standing in front of the judges' table.

"Keep up, twinster, you're competing on a dance show. You danced with your partner in the finals, you're being judged. Ready to hear their comments and your scores?"

I nod.

"Let's start with Carlo."

Carlo is the most mellow I've ever seen him. "That was magical, ethereal. The lifts were effortless, the musicality was magnificent. I'm speechless."

Mary Ann truly is speechless and motions for Glen to speak.

"Sophie, I've watched you dance since you were a little girl. You're extremely talented. What I saw here tonight was the best I've ever seen you dance. I know it's not ballroom, but there was emotion and connection that's so rare. Did you do the choreography?"

I nod.

"Do more. All of your dances this season have been beautifully choreographed. You have a gift."

When the judges raise their paddles, they're all tens. Which I expected. What I didn't expect was for the screen above the stage to light up and show the arena where the Devil Birds are playing two blocks away. The crowd is waving and cheering and, as if choreographed, a sea of paddles with the number ten written on them are raised high in the air, and both teams are giving us stick taps. Apparently stick taps are applause in hockey.

"They took a time-out to watch your performance at the game," Ian explains before turning back into a show host. "Now that the performances are done, and we have the judges' scores, it's time for the audience to vote!"

The numbers to text in votes for each couple flash on the screen, as does the website to vote online. We go to commercial break, and it's pandemonium getting ready for the announcement of the winners.

"I love you, Trevor. Thank you for this. How did you pull it off?" I ask from our spot offstage.

"Ian coordinated it. I was dancing with you come hell or high water, but we weren't sure of the logistics with the game. I meant it when I said you come first. I love my team, but not like I love you. If I had the flu, they could replace me with half a dozen other players. I'm hoping you find me irreplaceable." The kiss he gives me is tender.

"I do." Realizing what I said, I laugh. "But not for another ten years or so."

"I'm fine with that. Just save your last dance for me."

We're called on stage, and the results are announced. Trevor and I come in second to a teenage social media influencer with a huge following. I don't even care. The Platinum Paw trophy would've clashed with the décor of the pool house, anyway. The more important victory is that the Devil Birds win by a point and are keeping their playoff hopes alive.

Somehow the finale after-party merges with the Devil Birds' victory party, so it's a bar full of dancers and hockey players, family and friends. And I fit in. With all of them. I've gone from feeling like an outsider to being part of a community. Of multiple communities. So many of the dancers told me our dance was the best one and if it wasn't for the power of the teen influencer's mega fans we would've won. We should've won. They want me to choreograph dances on the summer tour. Not just group dances, but spotlight solos too.

The hockey players have been hugging me, and it feels like I gained a dozen new brothers. Not that I needed more brothers, but I'm touched by the way they rallied around Trevor and supported him throughout this whole experience. Supported us. Not once did I sense resentment or hostility from the team over the distraction Trevor dancing caused.

"Are you disappointed you didn't win?" Miranda asks, handing me a glass of champagne. I look around the room. I'm reunited with my best friend, something I didn't think was possible even a few months ago. My parents are at a table with Teagan, talking about something she's showing them on her phone, all three of them nodding and smiling. Trevor's laughing with his teammates and shoots me a sexy wink when he sees me watching him.

"Who says I didn't?" I ask before taking a sip.

EPILOGUE – SOPHIE

I'm having a blast traveling North America with the *Celebrity Dance Dare* contingent for the summer tour. Pros and contestants from the shifter and human shows are performing in cities all around the United States and Canada. It's amazing how enormous the US is and how different it is. I've traveled through Europe and the UK, but it doesn't prepare you for the vastness of the prairies. Many of our miles are covered in buses, so I'm seeing firsthand the variety of experiences the US offers.

Trevor joins me for most stops, only missing out when he's teaching at hockey camps. Whenever possible, he tries to hook up with hockey clinics in the towns we're performing in. He loves the camps with the younger kids who are still playing because it's the most fun. The camps for older kids with professional aspirations are more serious and competitive. The pressure the kids feel to be perfect weighs on him. He hasn't said anything, but I think he felt similar pressure growing up to gain his parents' attention and approval.

We're halfway through the tour, just another two weeks to go, and then we'll have a month off before the next show cycle starts. This is when they start offering contracts for the next season. They offered Scott, the winning pro from this past season, a contract yesterday, but I haven't heard anyone else saying they received an offer.

I'm settling into the hotel in Omaha, Nebraska when there's a knock on my door. Trevor has a key since we always share, so I check the peephole. It's Geoffrey, the head producer.

"Hey, Geoffrey, how are you?" I ask, stepping back to invite him into the room. It's a suite, so there's a seating area and a separate bedroom. It would've been creepy entertaining my boss a few feet from my bed. He's a meerkat shifter, so if I needed to shift and defend myself, my wolf would easily win. Or I'd cast a freeze spell on him. I'm not defenseless, which is something I don't take for granted. Not that I'd need to have to defend myself from Geoffrey, he's always been a perfect gentleman, but it's always good to know I could if necessary.

"I'm well, Sophie, how about you? Are you enjoying life on tour?" He takes a seat in the chair I offer him.

I sit on the sofa across from him. He's carrying a folder. Is that my pro contract? My hands are shaking, so I clasp them in my lap.

"I am. It's exciting to see so much of the United States. When I traveled with the Devil Birds, we flew most places, so I didn't experience it the same way. Flying first class wins over a tour bus, hands down, but at least I can say I did it."

"Hi, honey, I'm home," Trevor says as he lets himself into our suite. He stops short and flushes when he sees Geoffrey sitting there.

Geoffrey chuckles. "Hi, Trevor. We're planning for next season and working on our casting decisions."

"Oh." Trevor looks toward me with raised eyebrows. He knows what this may mean. "I didn't mean to interrupt. I'll be in the bedroom."

Reaching out, I grab his hand as he walks by.

"Join us. Is that okay, Geoffrey? He can hear anything you say to me."

"Absolutely."

With a nod, Trevor sits next to me on the sofa. His warm, solid presence is like an emotional hot water bottle, bringing me comfort and relaxing me.

Geoffrey clears his throat, then speaks. "We loved having you both on the past season of the shifter version of *Celebrity Dance Dare*, and we want to offer Sophie a contract as a professional partner on the main *Celebrity Dance Dare*. Your partner may be human. Probably will be human, unless they're a very famous shifter. Everything is outlined in the contract, but in a nutshell, you'll make more per episode, earn bonuses the longer your celebrity lasts in the competition, and it's a longer season."

He hands me the folder, and I keep my hand still long enough to grasp it.

"Have your attorney or agent review it. Our attorney's card is inside in case there are questions."

This is it. What I've dreamed of. What I've worked so hard for. I did it. Twin waves of pride and elation wash over me. Trevor's hand squeezes my knee.

"Oh, Sophie, I'm so proud of you!" He kisses my cheek. That's okay, we'll have contract celebration sex later.

A calmness settles over me. I know what I want.

"Geoffrey, thank you so much. I'm honored to be selected as a professional partner for CDD. However, I won't be negotiating this contract." I hand him back the folder, and he looks at me, startled.

Trevor gasps. "Soph, what are you doing?" He lowers his voice. "This is your dream."

I turn to him and smile. "It *was* my dream. I have a new dream now." Facing Geoffrey again, I continue. "Geoffrey, the contract I'd like to negotiate is as a member of the troupe and choreographer. Whatever the standard rate is. I don't want to be a professional partner. I'm not well suited to it, and I don't enjoy it."

At Trevor's sharp intake of breath, I giggle and pat his knee reassuringly.

"Of course, I enjoyed it with you, Trevor, but that's because I fell

in love with you. I won't be falling in love with any of my other partners, so it won't be fun."

"Damn well better not fall in love with anyone else," Trevor
mutters.

"I love performing, and I love choreographing, and I know I have
a talent for both. I'm too harsh as a teacher, and I don't have the
patience. The celebrities will have a miserable time with me as a
partner, and I don't want to ruin what should be a fun experience for
them."

"I'm sure that's not true!" Geoffrey protests.

Trevor scrunches up his face. "It's actually pretty self-aware and
accurate. She's a beautiful tyrant, but she's still a tyrant. Even when
she loves you."

"Is that something that would be possible, Geoffrey?" I don't
know what I'm going to do if it's not. I want to dance and be
involved in the show, but I don't want the time and possible travel
commitment being a pro partner demands. It's not just about not
being able to spend as much with Trevor if I'm a pro partner. I'm not
making this decision because of him. He's just a bonus. I'm making
this decision because it's what I want for myself and what is best for
me. I've spoken with Mom about the choices she made in her dance
career and life in general, and I realize I was looking at them from my
own perspective as a child and a teenager. As a grown woman, I can
see beyond what I thought she was giving up and recognize the
things she gained. My choices are different than hers, of course, but
I'm grateful to have her as an example of what a strong woman
making choices looks like."

Geoffrey nods his head vigorously. "Absolutely! We'd be thrilled
to have you in any capacity you want. There may be opportunities to
host or judge in the future if that's something you think you'd like to
pursue. You know the saying is 'If I'm not pro, I'm no' when it comes
to contracts, so I didn't consider offering you anything else. I'll get
our attorneys to draw up the alternate contract and get it to you in
the next couple of days."

He rises from his chair and holds out his hand for me to shake. He shakes Trevor's too for good measure, before exiting our suite.

"Gee," Trevor says as the door closes behind Geoffrey's retreating figure. "If only you knew someone with a specific interest in contract law who interned with agents while in law school who could review your contract to make sure it was okay."

"If only," I say wistfully as I trail a finger down his chest. "If they were pro bono, it would be even better."

I unbutton his shorts and slip my hand inside his boxer briefs.

We spend the rest of the afternoon enjoying the benefits of pro bono.

Did you enjoy Trevor and Sophie's story? Want a peek into their future? Get a bonus scene by subscribing to my mailing list at this link. https://dl.bookfunnel.com/fhto9qxsoa

ALSO BY JENNY FENSHAW

KEEP IN TOUCH!

Follow Jenny now for her romantic stories, stay for her ridiculous personality.

Warning: Snort laughing possible.

If you'd like to keep in touch with Jenny Fenshaw check out Jenny's website for all the ways to connect

https://jennyfenshaw.com/
Or just scan the QR code!

ABOUT THE AUTHOR

Jenny Fenshaw is a funny, goofy, and creative author of contemporary paranormal romantic comedies who loves daydreaming about ordinary events, making them ridiculous, and including them in her stories. A native of southern New Jersey, Jenny loves to set her stories in the area she knows so well. From the Atlantic City Boardwalk to the Pine Barrens, her stories are a love letter to her hometown just as much as they are the love story of her characters.

When she's not writing, Jenny enjoys watching ice hockey (for research!) and reruns of *Murder, She Wrote.* She has been married to her cinnamon roll of a husband for thirty years and has a grown son who has the best adventures.

www.ingramcontent.com/pod-product-compliance
Lightning Source LLC
Chambersburg PA
CBHW032002240626
47153CB00003B/1091